SINFUL

Novels by Marie Rochelle
Published by Phaze Books

Alpha Male Incorporated: Under Your Protection
Alpha Male Incorporated: Access Granted
A Taste of Love: Richard
Closer to You: Lee
My Deepest Love: Zack
More Than Friends: Brad
Caught
Caught 2: Ajana's Return
Desire
All the Fixin'
Crossing the Railroad
A Rancher's Promise
The Men of CCD: Slow Seduction
The Men of CCD: Loving True
The Men of CCD: Help Wanted
Lucky Charms
Hunks: Too Hot to Touch
Hunks: Opposite Attraction
Hunks: Pulled Over
Me & Mrs. Jones
Taken by Storm
Tempting Turner
Roped Into You
So Much Better
Bikers & Bars: Dante's Way

SINFUL

MARIE ROCHELLE

East Baton Rouge Parish Library
Baton Rouge, Louisiana

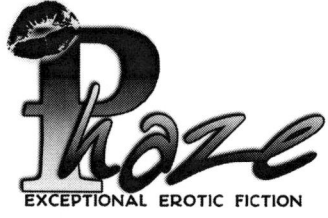

EXCEPTIONAL EROTIC FICTION

Sinful Copyright © 2013 by Marie Rochelle
ALL RIGHTS RESERVED.

Edited by Judy Bagshaw
Cover Art © 2013 by Skyla Dawn Cameron

First Edition August 2013
Trade Paperback ISBN: 978-1-60659-735-4
eBook ISBN: 978-1-60659-706-4

Published by Phaze Books
An imprint of Celeritas Unlimited LLC
6457 Glenway Ave., #109
Cincinnati, OH 45211

All rights reserved under the International and Pan-American Copyright Conventions. No part of this book may be reproduced or transmitted in any form or by any means, electronic or mechanical including photocopying, recording, or by any information storage and retrieval system, without permission in writing from the publisher, Celeritas Unlimited LLC, 6457 Glenway Avenue, #109, Cincinnati, Ohio 45211, books@mundania.com.

This book is a work of fiction. Names, characters, places and incidents are either the product of the author's imagination or are used fictitiously, and any resemblance to any actual persons, living or dead, events, or locales is entirely coincidental. The publisher does not have any control over and does not assume any responsibility for author or third-party websites or their content.

Legal File Usage—Your eBook Rights
Payment of the download fee for the ebook edition of this book grants the purchaser the right to download and read this file on any devices the purchaser owns, and to maintain private backup copies of the file for the purchaser's personal use only. It is a violation of copyright law for the purchaser to share or redistribute the ebook edition of this book to anyone who has not purchased the eBook.

The unauthorized reproduction or distribution of this or any copyrighted work is illegal. Authors are paid on a per-purchase basis. Any use of this file beyond the rights stated above constitutes theft of the author's earnings. File sharing is an international crime, prosecuted by the United States Department of Justice Division of Cyber Crimes, in partnership with Interpol. Criminal copyright infringement, including infringement without monetary gain, is punishable by seizure of computers, up to five years in federal prison and a fine of $250,000 per reported instance. Please purchase only authorized electronic or print editions and do not participate in or encourage the electronic piracy of copyrighted material. Your support of the author's rights and livelihood is appreciated.

Production by Celeritas Unlimited LLC
Printed in the United States of America
10   9   8   7   6   5   4   3   2   1

Dedication:

To Jonathan W.,
Thank for you making Saturday mornings so
magical for me.

Chapter One

"I can't believe that woman actually moved next door to my business," Jensen Lowe complained, glaring out of his office window at the dark blue car parked on the street. "It has taken me years to build up my client list. I'm not about to have everything ruined because of her."

"Don't you think that you're overacting just a little? Do you really believe her small business is going to take away all of our clients?" his brother argued. "Neither one of you are doing the same thing so neither one should interfere with the other. Just leave it alone."

Turning away from the window, Jensen gave his baby brother, Casper, a disapproving glance. "Why aren't you more upset about Sinful? Don't you know what she is going to do to us or don't you care?"

Casper propped his feet on the edge of his desk because he knew how much his brother hated it. Sometimes, Jensen wondered how he and his brother were even related because they were so dissimilar from each other. He planned for the future while Casper didn't see past the moment he was living in each and every day.

"Yes, I care about Fitness 24 but I highly doubt anyone here will get sidetracked by our new neighbor's bakery. So why don't you calm down and just let her do her thing?" Casper sighed. "I mean it's a little shop. I actually think it's pretty cute. I noticed some treats through the window and they did look enticing."

Coming across the room, Jensen knocked his brother's feet off his clean desk. "How about you let me handle this? You need to get downstairs to your next class before you're late again. I've gotten several complaints from clients last week about you."

Sighing, Casper got up from his seat. "No one in my class should have run and told you anything about me. I know how to do my job and if I didn't they wouldn't keep coming back three days a week," he complained. "It wasn't like I was an hour late; I mean it was only like five minutes late. Why were they acting like the world is coming to an end or something?"

"Your regulars aren't paying to stand there and stare at the walls while you take your sweet time doing whatever you were doing. They want to spend the entire hour learning kickboxing and nothing else," Jensen replied. "You keep asking for a bigger place to teach them, but how can I trust you with it? You aren't the most responsible person in the world."

Jensen pondered how much longer he could put up with his brother's immature attitude about life and their family business. He truly had about enough dealing with Casper's constant mistakes and screw ups over the last several weeks. He could hardly count on his sibling to be there for him anymore. It was like he was going solo with Fitness 24 instead of it being a partnership.

"God Jensen, take a breath and calm down. You're making life way too hard on yourself. Get out of this office more and live a little. Why don't you start teaching another class to burn off all of that energy? Because I know you aren't about to get a girlfriend since you haven't been out on a real date in over two years," Casper said, watching him. "I thought Chloe was a snot and bitch, but she got you out of this office. You need to get a woman or at least a female with benefits. You are way too tense to be so young."

He didn't need or want any kind of advice from his lack of commitment brother. It wasn't any of Casper's concern when he decided to start dating again. So, it would be for the best if he stayed out of his personal life and stuck to what he knew the best which was much *nothing*.

"Casper, you need to go and I do mean right this second before I say something I will regret later," Jensen warned.

"Alright, I'm gone but don't bother our new neighbor. She had a right to move next door. There isn't a law against it even if you think there should be. Please don't make it out to be more than it is." Turning around, Casper walked out of the room, but left his unwanted advice lingering behind.

Jensen blew off what his brother told him and then strolled back over to the huge bay window. He caught his neighbor as she went back to the trunk of her car. She grabbed more and more boxes from the trunk and carried them into the bakery next door. He still couldn't comprehend why the asshole property owner wouldn't sell the empty space to him, but sold it to someone like her.

What was this guy's deal anyway? Did the guy have a problem with him or something?

How would anyone at Fitness 24 succeed with this woman next door selling those high calorie treats? So many people would be too tempted not to break the rules.

His new neighbor had been open for almost six months, but he might be able to 'convince' her into finding a new location. Hell, he would even offer to buy the rest of the lease from her. He was planning to offer her so much money that she wouldn't be able to turn him down for any reason.

Knowing he wasn't going to get anything done unless he confronted Little Miss Sugar and Spice, Jensen eased away from the window and then walked out of his office door praying luck would be on his side.

✧

Dipping the spoon into the batter, Maymi Monroe tasted her grandmother's recipe for red velvet cupcakes one last time to make sure it gave her memories from her childhood. She wasn't about to bake and put anything in the display case if it wasn't totally satisfying for her customers.

The flavors were beyond perfection. She knew her grandmother would be so proud of her. Maymi laid the spoon to the side and picked up the ice cream scoop which belonged to her late grandmother. She wanted to do everything she could to keep the memory of her alive in her heart and mind.

She started filling up the paper-lined cupcake pans and was halfway through when the bell chimed above the entrance door. More and more, she was beginning to realize that she really needed to hire a morning person to work the counter. A majority of her money went right back into the business and supplies so much that all she could afford was a part-time woman student to work in the afternoons.

"Hello, is anyone here?" a voice called out.

"I'm coming," Maymi hollered, wiping her hands on her apron.

She hurried out of the kitchen door and literally stopped in her tracks when her eyes landed on the man standing there waiting for her.

Tall, dark and *handsome...* those three well-known words couldn't begin to even describe the hunk staring at her.

Short, jet-black hair covered his head, showing off his strong face along with his chiseled jaw line. The slight shadow of his beard gave him an even more striking look, but it didn't take away from the hint of a dimple in his chin.

He stood there as if he prided himself on his good looks. She couldn't deny how acutely aware she was of this guy's beautifully proportioned body. He had an innately captivating presence that seemed to fill her entire bakery.

Maymi was surprised to find a guy like him inside of her shop. He didn't look like he did anything but work out and eat protein bars. Why would he step out of the gym and walk inside here? However, if he had a sweet tooth, she wasn't about to turn away a sale, not with the mortgage she had to pay on this place.

His tawny brown eyes raked over her body then came back up to study her face. Maymi couldn't help but wonder why he was staring at her so intently. He was coming off as a little defensive and for the life of her she couldn't figure out the reason why. This was the first time she had even laid eyes on him. She hadn't done anything to him.

"Hi, I'm Maymi Monroe. May I help you with something, sir?" She smiled, walking closer to the glass display counter.

"I own the gym next door and I came over here to see how you got this place instead of me," the guy questioned, his tone harsh. "I offered the realtor a huge sum of money and I constantly got shot down. How did someone like you get a yes from that jerk?"

At first, Maymi glanced around looking for a hidden camera because she sure in the hell better be getting punk'd since this guy better not be seriously asking how someone 'like her' got this shop.

Was he out of his damn mind?

"Excuse me. Did I hear you correctly?" Maymi asked, hoping she truly had misunderstood him. No one could actually be this damn disrespectful intentionally.

"I believe I spoke quite clearly, but I can repeat myself if you need me to," he said, staring at her.

Maymi's eyebrows shot up as she tried to tamp down her anger.

How dare this man come inside her place of business and speak to her like this! She had worked too damn hard to get here to get slighted by him or anyone else for that matter.

"Listen, sir," she replied. "You better leave now before I lose my temper. If you can't find your way out, I'll be more than happy to show you the door."

"My name is Jensen Lowe...not sir, and you didn't answer my question," he tossed back at her. "What person in their right mind would open a bakery next door to a twenty-four hour fitness club? It doesn't make any sense. I think you need to pack up your things and move."

Maymi was so taken back by Jensen's startling suggestion that she was at a loss for words, but they came rushing back to her. "Either you are stupid or the most self-centered man I've had the misfortune to ever meet, but I don't care about what you think or say. All I want you to do is get the hell out of my bakery."

Storming around the corner of the display case, Maymi stood in front of Jensen. She tried not to notice how good he smelled up close or how his eyes seemed to be staring straight through her. His ass was going to leave her building one way or another, the choice was up to him.

"Get out," she demanded, again.

Surprise etched across his handsome face as he stared down at her from his towering six feet five inch frame. "I'm not done speaking with you yet. I need to say a few more things," Jensen told her.

"Oh, you are done whether you know it or not, Mr. Lowe."

Storming past him, Maymi went over to the bakery's door, flinging it wide open. "You can leave now," she said, waving him out. "Be sure not to come back here again because I won't be so nice the next time I see you."

Jensen stared at her a few seconds before he sauntered towards the door. He paused in front of her and waited like he thought she might change her mind about kicking him out of her store. Well, it would be a cold day in hell before that happened.

"You only need to walk about five more feet and you will be outside where I want you, Mr. Lowe." Maymi glanced at the sidewalk then back at him.

"This conversation isn't over, Ms. Monroe," he promised before turning around and storming out the door.

"Oh, that is your misconception but not mine. I'm not ever going to be in a room alone with you again," Maymi snapped before letting go of the door watching as it slowly closed in Jensen Lowe's face.

Turning on her heel, she marched back into her kitchen, wondering how such a rude and disrespectful man had the ability to run a gym in the first place. Shouldn't a person over a people driven business like his have a better personality?

How could someone like him show empathy towards a struggling client who might not be able to lose weight fast enough?

Well, he wasn't any of her concern anymore.

Thank God she belonged to a gym way on the other side of town. If not, she might not be responsible for her actions if she was inside the same work out facility that Mr. Lowe owned.

Chapter Two

"How dare she kick me out of her bakery like I wasn't worth her time," Jensen snapped minutes later, storming into his office as the door slammed behind him. He had gone over to Sinful hoping to talk with that woman like two adults, but instead Ms. Monroe had acted like a spoiled brat and then tossed him out on the sidewalk.

If she believed he was done with her then she was out of her mind. He wasn't going to let her treat him like his concerns weren't important. She could deny the truth all she wanted, but her bakery, with its fattening goodies, would ruin the progress his members were trying to make.

For the time being, he wouldn't go back over there and confront Ms. Monroe again, but he wasn't going to back down. One thing was for sure, she hadn't let him intimidate her. She might have been barely five feet three inches, but for what his neighbor lacked in height she sure made up for it in backbone.

Walking around his office, Jensen thought about another way to approach her. From the way Maymi acted towards him at Sinful, she wasn't going to box up her mixing bowls and go anywhere which wasn't going to work for him. She had to leave and he didn't care how it happened, just as long as it did.

"Fuck," he cursed, storming over to his desk and taking a seat behind it. He still couldn't figure out how she ended up with that prime piece of property.

The money amount he had offered the real estate agent was three times what it was worth and his expansion depended on that building. He couldn't move forward without it. He owed it to the people who paid his membership fee to see that Ms. Monroe wasn't around much longer to cause them any kind of setback.

Who in their right mind wanted a bakery shop in the neighborhood anyway?

All of those calories and of course fat was horrible for anyone's body. Casper might think it was fine she moved next to them, but he didn't and never would. All of her tempting, delicious smelling products were going to be a bad temptation to his clients.

Reaching for his phone on the desk, Jensen dialed his real estate broker's phone number because he was going to get down to the bottom of this situation.

"Jensen, what can I do for you?" Paul Williams answered on the second ring.

"Paul, can you tell me how in this hell this woman Maymi Monroe got the building next door to Fitness 24? I offered a huge amount of money for it but the agent shot me down. I don't think he even took five minutes to even think about it."

"We've been over this before." Paul sighed. "Mr. Banks didn't want the walls knocked down from your business and have it expanding over into his space. I knew as soon as you saw the new owner you would call me."

Jensen swallowed hard, attempting to control his anger. *Nothing* was going his way today and now he had to deal with this nonsense. He couldn't wrap his head around the stupidity of it.

"Do you know what the new owner turned the empty space into?" he demanded harshly.

"No, I don't but I bet you're going to tell me," Paul replied with a hint of sarcasm in his voice.

"A bakery," Jensen snapped. "How in the hell does that make any sense? One of my members will work on losing calories and then can go right next door and regain them in a matter of minutes after eating a red velvet cupcake."

Paul's deep voice laughed in his ear, making him pull it away. He glared at it, not finding one thing funny about this at all. Something had to be done, he just didn't know what it was, but he would figure it out.

"It isn't funny," he snapped, placing the phone back against his ear.

"Sorry Jensen." Paul coughed, clearing his voice. "But you have to admit there is some humor in the situation. You need to loosen up. Fitness 24 is not going to lose any of it members nor will they gain twenty pounds because of Ms. Monroe's bakery. Let her know the feeling of success like you did when your gym first took off.

"Listen, if you're so determined to expand your business, have you thought about looking into that old Armory over on Griffith Avenue? It's been abandoned for months. I can probably get the keys to it for a walk through."

The idea of opening a second work-out club in the area hadn't crossed his mind, but he didn't have the time to make a list of the pros and cons right now. There were more pressing matters needing his attention and until he had that taken care of, the second health club would have to be put on hold.

"Let me think about it and I'll get back to you," Jensen answered.

"Don't wait too long. It's the perfect space for what you want done and it will give you the extra space for the karate class you talked about starting," Paul told him and then hung up.

Jensen placed the phone back into its cradle. He leaned back into his leather chair and spun around so he could look out the window of his office.

He wasn't going to need to think about buying a second building because he wasn't going to need it. He never lost a battle and a five feet three inch brown beauty wasn't going to be his first defeat either.

Chapter Three

"I can't believe the nerve of that man," Maymi mumbled to herself, tossing the spatula into the soapy sink water.

Jensen Lowe had walked into her place of business making demands like he owned the building instead of her. How in the hell could she have gotten sidetracked by his attractive face?

Well, his shitty attitude made his good looks go downhill quite fast. He actually implied she wasn't good enough to be an entrepreneur like him. What in the fuck was he thinking? She could do anything he could and probably ten times better.

Walking over to the table, Maymi opened the drawer searching through it until she found her favorite plastic spatula. She liked using this one when she did her red velvet cupcakes since the icing seemed to go on smoother.

Thankfully, the display case out front was almost completely full since she had come in three hours early today. All of her delicious treats were out there looking tempting and mouth watering.

She could start working on getting all of her cookies and pies together for the extra display case she had placed on the other side of her bakery. A variety of items to choose from would bring in more money for her.

She wasn't going to allow Sinful to fail for any reason. For almost six years, she worked at a variety of diverse jobs that she hated to save up money for her dream bakery in the city. *Sinful* was her heart and soul. Nothing or no one was *ever* going to take this away from her.

Heading back over to the tray of cupcakes, Maymi opened the white container of homemade cream cheese frosting before picking up a cool cupcake off the rack next to her. Slowly, she started icing the delectable treat, making sure not to get any crumbs into the frosting.

These were her bestsellers anytime she made them back in her hometown. They usually sold out in an hour or less, so she didn't doubt they would do well for her here as well.

Maymi continued working while she thought about the triple chocolate fudge cupcakes she had been working on as well. Something was keeping them from getting moist like she wanted and for some odd reason she couldn't figure out what it was. It was out of her reach, taunting her to keep fixing the recipe until she got it perfect enough to put out there to sell.

If her grandmother was still alive, her nana would be able to just take a small bite and instantly know what was wrong with them. Her bakery couldn't be successful if only one of her cupcakes sold like hot cakes. She needed everything to come together like a dessert lovers' naughty fantasy.

Finishing off the last cupcakes, Maymi laid the utensil down and picked up the tray carrying it back through the swinging door. She worked on filling up the second shelf on her case, hoping customers would come in and buy everything out.

Since her grand opening six months ago, she had noticed a steady flow of customers coming through the door, but she wanted more than she was getting. She needed at least a twelve to fifteen percent increase or she wouldn't survive on those kinds of sales; however, she was positive once word got out about how scrumptious her baked goods were, she wouldn't be able to keep the cases filled.

Placing the tray down near the cash register, Maymi walked around the front of the case to get a better look at everything. All of them looked very enticing, but the counter itself was unappealing.

Tonight, when she was at home, she would sketch out a design for the front window and the counter as well. Sinful was missing a logo to set it above the rest of the businesses on this block. She needed something more than good smelling desserts to make an individual stop and come inside. She had to make something eye catching enough from the outside to draw them into her world of goodies.

If she accomplished that one huge thing then her business was finally going to make her father respect her decision to drop out of medical school and pursue her own dreams not his personal visions for her.

After her mother's sudden suicide when she was a little girl, she worked hard to constantly prove herself to her father since he expected so much from his youngest child. He might own a successful medical practice, but she could be equally successful if he only had more belief in her skills as a baker.

However, nothing she did ever seemed good enough for Doctor Raymond Monroe. She could have earned two medical degrees and he would have still found something to criticize her about over and over again.

More than anything she wanted to gain her father's love and respect. Yet, all of his titles hanging up on his office wall meant more to him than her or anything she had accomplished over the past several years.

He would rather do something with her older brothers because they shared the same interests and circle of friends. They could never do anything wrong in his eyes. Her brothers always treated her with love and respect; they even came to help her pack up her things to move out here. Yet, they didn't seem to understand how their father loved them more than her and sadly they probably never world.

None of the cooking awards she won over the past two years would hold a candle to hearing those words. Yet, her father cared more about prestige and status to ever come to any of the cooking shows she participated in.

Blinking back sudden tears, Maymi took one last look at the cupcake case before going back around the counter and picking up the tray she had left there.

Damn Jensen Lowe for coming into her business and making her think about her failed relationship with her father. She hadn't heard from him since she packed up and left Savannah, Georgia to move out here.

Of course, he wouldn't call to check on her because she had broken his heart by not wanting to take over his medical business. Her older brother, Broderick, finally agreed to step up and do it. Once he did, Dr. Monroe disowned her with a snap of his fingers and never looked back at his only daughter.

Going back into the other room, Maymi walked over to the sink and added the dirty trays to the dishes already soaking there and started washing them to ease her mind. All of the manual labor would have to be done by her but she didn't care. Whatever she had to do to help accomplish her ultimate goal would be done because she relished in creating something that was all hers.

Her father thought she hadn't inherited anything from him, but he was wrong. She got a very important quality—discipline. She made a plan a long time ago to own her own bakery and had stuck to it no matter what obstacles had been tossed in her way.

Why he couldn't understand this, she would never know.

However, Jensen wasn't something she had been expecting but she wasn't going to let him get her off track proving a point to her father. She was good enough…no great enough…to make Sinful one of the top bakeries in the city.

After she finished with the dishes, Maymi placed the last utensil in the sink to dry. Since the cupcakes were done, it was time for her to start working on the crust for her pecan, apple and cherry pies. All three had won first place at different baking shows and contests. Therefore why wouldn't she have them at her own shop?

Who didn't want a sweet treat when something happened like a bad breakup or loss?

She wanted to lure all of those customers through her door with a cupcake or a hot slice of pie. Both of them always took the blues away for her during those times. Which is probably why she had the curves she did instead of being slimmer like Tatum was, but she didn't let that bother her much anymore.

Regardless of what her cranky neighbor thought of her being so 'close' to his personal space, she wasn't going anywhere and she would love to see him try to make her.

Chapter Four

"Jensen, what's wrong with you? You haven't spoken three words to me since you picked me up for our date."

Looking across the table at his favorite Chinese restaurant, he stared at his on and off girlfriend Chloe glaring at him. He hadn't wanted to stay at home tonight because he didn't want to think about Maymi ruining his business, so he called her up without thinking it through.

Her whiny personality was one of the top reasons he stopped dating her before. She had a very bad habit of always making things so much bigger than they were. Furthermore, if all of the attention wasn't directed at her, she felt like something was wrong and complained like a little girl. His life was filled with too much conflict to be stroking her shallow ego.

"Chloe, I have a lot on my mind," he finally answered, cursing his spilt second decision to call her.

"Please don't tell me it's about that gym of yours. I think you worry about that place way too much. You're doing well with it. My friends are always bragging about how amazing your instructors are there. What else do you want?" she complained. "Aren't you satisfied with what you have?"

"Fitness 24 is more than a business to me, Chloe. It's my blood, sweat and tears. I've been working for years to get it where it is today. Besides my brother Casper, you're the next person who should know how much it means to me. Why do you still have such a problem with it?" he demanded.

Sighing, Chloe flipped her curly brown hair over her shoulder before reaching across the table and grabbing his hand, brushing her thumb over the top.

"I'm sorry, baby. Can I do something to make it up to you?" She leaned forward showing off the huge amount of cleavage displayed by the deep opening in the front of her shirt.

In the past, his cock would have already been rock hard just from her touch, but he figured out Chloe's game a while ago. She flirted with men when she figured out she was on the losing end of the argument. She loved getting her way and she used anything, including sex, to get it.

Jensen eased his hand away from her. Shit, he would make sure not to make this error in his thinking again. Being lonely was a way lot better than fighting off Chloe's high sexual needs. He was surprised she wasn't dating someone with the way she loved sex.

"No, that's alright." He sighed. "How about we just finish up our meal and then I can take you back home? I need to get up early to teach a class for Casper."

Snatching her hand back from him, Chloe fell back against her chair and crossed her toned, tanned arms over her surgically enhanced breasts. She narrowed her hazel eyes at him, but he didn't flinch under her cold stare.

"If you weren't interested in going back to my place after dinner why did you invite me here? We never stayed together because we had long, meaningful conversations."

He wanted to deny with Chloe was telling him but he couldn't. The only reason he asked her out was because of her killer body when he saw her working out at Fitness 24 for a body building competition. His first thought only consisted of how good she was going to look on his arm because she wasn't overly muscular but she was perfectly in shape like one of the female diva wrestlers from WWE.

"You're right," he admitted. "We both loved the hot sex and being the best looking couple in the room. However, I thought maybe you might have matured a little since we last were a couple. I know I've grown up a lot."

Rolling her eyes, she unfolded her arms and picked up her purse from the side of the table. "Well, good for you, Jensen," she snapped. "I'm going to the bathroom so I can freshen up and instead of dropping me off at home you can take me to Raven's. I heard the live band there tonight is incredible."

Are you sure about that?" he asked. "Raven's is a tougher part of town."

Chloe shot him a disgusted look before getting up from her seat. "I will be fine, Dad. I know a couple of bouncers there. So, I'll be okay. Just be ready to leave when I get back."

Storming away from the table, Chloe made her way through the semi-crowded restaurant without looking back at him. Jensen quickly prayed for the guy that would get hooked by her tonight. She was in one of her moods and she wouldn't stop until she got what she wanted from the poor soul.

The only good thing that came out of tonight was Chloe's selfish personality got his mind temporarily off her. Maymi wasn't going to get underneath his skin anymore. If he could control his temper with his unmotivated brother Casper then there was no way Ms. Monroe shouldn't be a lot easier for him to handle.

All he had to do was find a way to make her understand that her bakery business Sinful might be a lot more profitable away from his gym.

If Sinful stayed located next door to Fitness 24, it wouldn't be good marriage between the two of them. Maymi might act like there was something unfair about his demands, but he had enough sense to know there wasn't a damn thing wrong with them.

She would feel the same way he did if a doughnut franchise suddenly moved in next door to her and slowly stole her customers away. She might not be strong enough to confront her competition, but he was he would keep doing it until she got the hint.

Taking a deep breath, Jensen blew it out through his nose, trying to get himself back under control. Usually, he wasn't bothered by small stuff, however after dealing with Maymi and then his mistake of adding Chloe into the mix he was about at the end of his rope. Nothing else could happen to make his night any worse, because all he wanted to do was get home and forget the events of today even happened.

The sounds of female laughter coming from his left drew Jensen's attention. After his horrible day, he wondered who in the hell could be having such a good time and if they would be able to share their secret with him.

Because he would give almost anything to have a good careful laugh right now to block out all of the craziness going in his world.

It was almost enough to make him regret opening up Fitness 24 in the first place.

Spinning around in his chair, Jensen's gaze searched the room until he stopped at a table of three African American women sitting off towards the corner. One of the women was a little bit on the curvier side and her dark black hair tumbled carelessly to her shoulders in a mass of natural curls showing off her dark mahogany skin.

The second was just as attractive with her lighter caramel complexion, but her straighter hair was pulled back into a tight ponytail that stopped right above her shoulder blades.

But the last female seated at the table held his attention the most. She made his earlier anger resurface with record speed. However, before he could glance away Maymi's big brown eyes looked up from her plate and found him watching her.

Her eyebrows shot up in surprise before they slanted down into a frown as she glared at him. She looked just as stunned to see him here as he was to see her.

Wonderful, he thought.

Jensen didn't think anything else could happen to piss him off before leaving the restaurant, but he was wrong. Little Miss Bakery had to show up at his favorite restaurant and completely ruin what little he had left of his already horrible day. Hell! He was beginning to wonder if he could go anywhere without her showing up.

Chapter Five

"I swear I hate that asshole," Maymi mumbled underneath her breath, tossing her fork back down on her half-eaten plate of food.

She came out with her two best friends to finally celebrate the opening of her bakery. Tatum had been out of town on business so she and Jazmaine decided to wait until tonight so they could all have a good time together.

"Who are you talking about?" Jazmaine Ramey said, turning around to look over her shoulder.

"Don't look," she whispered, grabbing her friend's arm. "I don't want him to think we're talking about him. He already has a big enough ego as it is."

Spinning back around, Jazmaine eased her arm away from her. "God, what has crawled up your ass and died? I thought this dinner tonight was supposed to be fun and relaxing, but you've been on edge ever since we picked you up at your house."

"I agree with Jazmaine," Tatum Barnes agreed, cutting in. "Who has rubbed you the wrong way?"

Looking past Jazmaine, Maymi tried not to roll her eyes as Jensen got up from his seat and left with a leggy brunette. Of course, he would be with someone as perfect as him. They probably ran in the same circle as other flawless people who never step foot in her bakery.

"Turn around and look at the tall guy leaving the dark-haired woman," she said, knowing she would regret telling her friends anything about Jensen.

Maymi hoped he would hurry up and leave so she wouldn't have to look at him anymore but he stopped at the door then stared at her one last time before going out of the door. Slowly, her best friends faced her again after Jensen was finally gone.

"Who in the hell was he?" Tatum gushed. "Did you see how gorgeous he was? I mean his face was perfect in every sense of the word. How could you call someone like him an asshole?"

"Maymi, you can't keep your connection to that sexy man a secret from us," Jazmaine complained. "You know that we will keep asking you until we break you down. Why go through all of that with us?"

Why did she ever open her mouth?

Maymi knew she should have kept quiet when she spotted Jensen staring in her direction. She had actually seen him right after the waitress seated them, but just kept her mouth shut.

"Maymi, are you paying any attention to us?"

"Yes, I hear you Jazmaine." She sighed. "I just don't want to talk about Jensen Lowe any more tonight. I've dealt with him enough today."

"He's the guy you told us about on the drive over here?" Tatum asked, shocked. "I can't believe it. How could you leave out how good he looked? I mean, I would love to do some baking with him and it wouldn't occur inside of the kitchen."

"You're supposed to be on my side, not drooling over my enemy," Maymi snapped, wondering how the conversation had gotten so sidetracked.

Tatum's light brown eyes lit up with mischief as her hand reached for her drink and then she took a sip. "What can I say?" she said. "You know I have a weakness for tall, handsome, physically fit white guys. Why do you think I work out at our local gym four days a week?"

"I thought it was to stay in shape because you love wearing those short skirts and high heels." Maymi grinned. "I don't have a clue how you keep up with all of the men you date. You seem to have them falling over their feet to ask you out on a date."

"I tell you it's the ponytail. Men have fantasies about pulling long hair while making love." Tatum grinned. "Why shouldn't I give them a little visual stimulation? It doesn't mean I'm going to let them get any."

"Okay, you two, enough of that," Jazmaine cut in. "I want to know how a guy who looks like that can be such a jerk? Is he serious about you moving your bakery away from his workout gym? He can't force you to do anything. I hope he knows that and takes a step back."

Maymi was positive that Jensen knew the law, but none of that meant he wasn't going to make her life a living hell. He was without a doubt going to be a pain in her side. No matter how gorgeous he might be on the outside, he was nasty and not worth another moment of her time. She was supposed to be having a good time, not plotting ways to get rid of him.

"How about we forget about Mr. Lowe and enjoy the rest of our dinner?" she suggested. "I have to be at work early to finish up three cupcake orders plus finish decorating a Hello Kitty special order cake for a five-year-old's birthday party."

"Can I ask you one more thing about him?" Tatum asked.

"No, you can't," she answered, tired of talking about Jensen. "I want to know what's going on with you two."

"Nothing as exciting as you have going on," Jazmaine answered then glanced down at her watch. "Damn, I have to go. I'm supposed to be back at work in twenty minutes for another board meeting."

"Are you serious?" Maymi asked, staring at her friend. "I thought you would at least be able to finish having dinner with us."

Jazmaine glanced away from her with a guilty expression on her face. "I know. I was hoping I could put off telling you until later, but I couldn't," she said, looking back at her. "You know we are merging the company I work for with another business that specializes in graphic novels. I swear this venture has lasted way too long. I want it to be done and over with."

"How much long will it take?" Maymi inquired. "It seems like it has been going on for months now."

Sighing, Jazmaine nodded her head. "It has been about four months now, but my boss keeps telling me the guy only has a few more requests before he'll sign the papers. God, I hope everything will be done in the next couple of weeks, but who knows. I think he's holding up things on purpose. I've heard he's a real hard ass when he doesn't get every single thing he wants. However, Mr. Akito Mashiro will learn very quickly that I don't like to play games. My time is *too* precious for him to be jerking me around for dumb stuff."

Maymi was glad she wasn't the only one dealing with a difficult man at the moment, but Jazmaine was luckier than her. The man causing her all of these problems wasn't in her face.

"I would gladly trade places with you because your headache isn't right next door and threatening to make you move out of a building he has absolutely no control over."

"Maymi, you're right but this guy is making me work way too much overtime because he can. I think my problem is a lot worse than yours," Jazmaine disagreed.

"Why don't you two stop complaining so we can have fun with what little time we have left before Jazmaine has to leave." Tatum sighed. "I know those comic books can wait another ten or fifteen minutes".

"Tatum, I've told you before that graphic novels aren't the same thing as comic books. They are longer and have a complete story from start to finish, instead of ending with a traditional cliffhanger regular comic books are known for.

"In addition, some graphic novels are unsuitable for young kids because they have more detailed illustrations with their sex and violence. If Mr. Mashiro signs with my boss, it would skyrocket Mr. Kent's name in the industry since this guy is known for his Manga style of novels."

"Okay, I get it," Tatum sighed, rolling her eyes making Maymi laugh. "Graphic novels are like the Nip/Tuck of the fiction world. So, I'm also guessing I couldn't walk by a newsstand and just pick one up."

"No, you can't," Jazmaine said. "Now can you stop picking on me and pretending that you don't know how important this deal is to me?"

"Sorry," Tatum apologized. "I only wanted to finish my meal and maybe talk one of you into going out with me for a little dancing tonight."

"How do you still have so much energy to do all of that?" Maymi complained. "I barely have enough get up and go to crawl out of bed now since opening up the bakery."

Taking a sip of her drink, Tatum eyed her a few minutes then shrugged her shoulders. "I don't know. Maybe it comes from being a yoga instructor on the weekends. I've all kinds of boundless energy nowadays. I told you that you should sign up for one of my classes at the gym."

For the past week, she had missed her lower abs workout classes. She better get back before she got too far behind and couldn't be able to do anything anymore. "Where would I fit in the time for an extra class? I already take two now and I can barely make those two on most days," Maymi answered.

"Do you really think the rumors are true and Jack is going to sell to another fitness place in town? I mean I've been going to the same place for six years," Tatum complained. "I'm not good with change. The thought of finding another place doesn't sit well with me. I like my gym being only a thirty minute drive from my back door."

Maymi was worried about losing their favorite workout spot as well. It held special memories for her since it was the place all of them had become friends. Meeting up there was a part of their routine. Even when one of them couldn't make it, the other two always found a way to show up. Now that Jazmaine was working as hard as her, it was harder for them to come together like they used to do in the past.

Everything around them seemed to be changing at such a rapid pace, but she couldn't let any of that take her focus away from the most important accomplishment she had going on. She was the proud owner of her own business. She had to keep that front and center in her mind or all of her hard work would have been for nothing.

"Ladies, let's not worry about any of this right now. Jack loves owning a gym and I doubt he'll let it go unless the money wasn't there to keep it open," she pointed out.

"You're right," Jazmaine agreed a second before her cell phone went off. She pulled it out of her purse and then cursed, tossing it back inside. "God, I really do hate Mr. Mashiro's assistant. She calls me like twenty times a day and I believe it's on purpose."

Maymi already guessed what Jazmaine was going to tell them before the words even left her mouth. "You have to leave, don't you?" she asked her girlfriend.

"Of course, I do. The assistant from hell just summons me back to the office. I swear if he wasn't the most sought after graphic novelist for our competitor, I would tell him to shove his pen where the sun doesn't shine."

"Don't lose your temper. You've worked too long to get this far with this guy. All you have to do is get him to sign the contract and you're done with him. At least, he's still in London and sending the message through his assistant."

"I know, but dealing with his demands is wearing on my one last nerve. I swear when I do finally lay eyes on him he might not like what comes out of my mouth."

"Since dinner didn't turn out good for any of us, how about we reschedule another one for next week," Tatum suggested. "I hate that you guys are having such a trying week when mine has been stress free. I can pay for this one since I got a little extra in my paycheck this week."

Maymi would love to do it, but she was booked solid for the next two weeks with orders for weddings, graduations and retirement parties. She wouldn't have any free time for anymore dinners for a while. Most of hers would be eaten at Sinful while icing a cake or while doing the baking for the next day.

"I'm sorry. I won't have any more free time for another dinner anytime soon. I'm swamped with orders for the next several weeks," she said, watching Tatum roll her eyes.

"Don't even say it, Tatum. I know I need to get out more but you know how much it means to me to make this a success. I have so much to prove."

She had taken out a huge loan to secure this bakery and she couldn't afford to miss one payment to the bank or owner of the property. Every single order that she got in had to be given the same amount of attention.

She couldn't get behind on any payments because not only would the bank give her problems, but also the property owner, who wouldn't think twice about taking his building back from her. Mr. Sajack only wanted the check placed inside of his hand and definitely allowed no excuses for a late payment.

"Don't worry about it," Maymi said. "I can pay for all of us. Why don't you give Tatum a ride back to work? I can get a cab. I'm going back to the bakery to finish up this cake order anyway."

Both Tatum and Jazmaine's eyes grew wide as saucers as they stared at her like she was out of her mind. "You can't go back to work at eight o'clock at night, are you crazy?" Tatum asked. "Just go back home and go to work early tomorrow morning. Nothing you have to do at Sinful is so important you have to be inside that building at night all alone."

Sighing, Maymi knew she wouldn't be able to change her girlfriend's mind about her going back to work. When Tatum spoke, she expected everyone to follow her rules without any kind of argument.

"Fine, I'll go home instead and work on putting my cake boxes together, but I'll have to be back there at five o'clock because I've two cakes that will go out within four hours of each other."

Tatum smiled at her, but didn't say a word. God, she hated when her bossy girlfriend got her way so easily. This was going to be the first and last time either one of her friends talked her out of going back to work no matter how late it might be.

"Great, I'm glad we're done with that," Jazmaine cut in. "Now, can let's pay the bill so I can get back to my ball and chain."

"You're right about that," Maymi teased, raising her hand for the waiter. "You are married to that job. All of us need to go on a long vacation."

"Do you really have time for fun in the sun on a tropical beach?" Jazmaine questioned, watching her as the waiter came back with their check.

Laughing, Maymi shook her head. "No, but a girl can dream," she answered, handing the waiter her credit card. "It's what keeps me going every night when I drag myself to bed after a long hard day at work."

"Hmmm...the only thing I would want to dream about is that delicious Jensen Lowe. You should think of a dessert and then name it after him." Tatum cut in, grinning at her.

Maymi caught herself before she literally fell out of her seat. There was no way anything named after that man would be placed on the inside of any of her bakery cases. Every treat was made with tender, loving care and nothing about him was tender or loving.

"How about you keep your baking ideas to yourself and let me handle the dessert world?" she suggested as the waiter came back with her credit card.

"Fine, but I think if you had him standing outside your bakery holding a tray of your famous red velvet cupcakes, you would have so many female customers that you wouldn't be able to handle the rush," Tatum tossed back at her.

"Alright, I hear you." She sighed, sliding her credit card back into her wallet. "How about we get out of here? I don't want Jazmaine's client's assistant calling her again."

Standing up, Maymi grabbed her coat off the back of her chair, watching as Tatum and Jazmaine did the same thing. She loved the closeness of their relationship because growing up with two older brothers she always wanted a sister to share her secrets with at night.

She never doubted her girlfriends wouldn't be there with her through thick and thin no matter what the problem was.

"He isn't my client yet," Jazmaine corrected as they walked away from the table heading for the front door. "I still need to stroke his assistant's ego along with his which is a tough thing to do since I've never laid eyes on the man."

"You're the best person for the job and when you win both of them over they will apologize for making you work so hard to get them to see what we already do. I'm so confident you will get Mr. Mashiro to sign those papers, I will have a party for you at my house," Maymi said.

Linking her arm hers, Jazmaine glanced down at her. "I will only celebrate if you promise to make me your famous triple layer carrot cake. I haven't eaten one in forever."

"Alright, I can do that for you," Maymi agreed.

She was the kind of friend that would be there for her friends no matter what they were experiencing. So if Jazmaine wanted her grandmother's blue ribbon triple layer carrot cake then she would have it.

Chapter Six

Early the following morning, Maymi grabbed the stack of bakery boxes out of the back of her car she had placed there last night after her dinner with Jazmaine and Tatum. They had Sinful across the top along with a cute design of a bakery in the background. She had them specially made to showcase her business and they weren't cheap, so she had to be very careful with them.

She tried working on little things like this at home, so she could spend more of her time working on new recipes for the bakery. The more she could work on improving would be one step closer to proving this career wasn't a mistake.

Holding the boxes against her chest, she stepped on the sidewalk trying to look around the side to make sure no one was coming. She prayed that she would make it to the front door before any of them accidentally hit the ground. She was about five steps away when a voice yelled.

"Ma'am, watch out!" a second before a hard body crashed into her sending her flying to the ground in one direction and the hot pink boxes in the other.

She didn't have time to brace herself before she fell on her ass. Thankfully, she had enough back there to protect her body, but she wasn't so sure her boxes were that lucky. She didn't even have to look at them to know they were damaged.

"God, are you alright? I'm so sorry. I was running and you stepped out in front of me so fast before I could stop," the guy apologized.

Brushing her hair out of her face, Maymi gasped as she stared into the bluest eyes she had ever seen. She couldn't even answer his question because she was so taken back by how good-looking he was.

"Here let me help you up," he said, grabbing her by the hand as people walked around them.

"Thanks," Maymi answered as a person kicked one of her boxes and kept on walking. She took a step back and wiped her hands down the front of her jeans. She looked around at the crushed boxes and cursed underneath her breath.

"Damn, they are all ruined. What in the hell am I going to do? I only have a few left inside the bakery"

"I'm so sorry about the boxes." He apologized again as he bent down and picked them up holding them out to her. "Is there anything I can do to help you? I feel so bad about this. I should have been paying better attention to where I was going."

"It's okay," she sighed. "I might have a few extra ones in the storage room that I can put together before my customers come in to pick up their cakes. My cupcakes orders aren't due until later in the afternoon and that is what these boxes are for."

"Show me what to do and I can put them together for you. I don't have to be at work for another hour and it's the least I can do since I ruined them."

Maymi looked at the gorgeous guy standing next to her and he looked so sincere but she knew nothing about him. How could she invite him into her bakery? He could be a killer for all that she knew.

"Hmmm...that's okay. I can get them done myself while the cupcakes are baking in the oven. I'm very good at multitasking."

Smiling, the guy stared at her for a few minutes. "I'm not a serial killer if that's what you're thinking. My brother would kill me if I embarrassed him anymore than I usually do. I swear I only want to help you out for messing up your gorgeous boxes. I'm really good with my hands. I'd have them done in no time. By the way, my name is Casper Lowe."

Maymi paused and did a double take. She couldn't believe what she was hearing. There was no way this guy and Jensen were brothers. They were like day and night even in the looks department.

"Is your brother the same Jensen Lowe, the man who owns the gym next door?" she asked.

"Yes, he is," Casper answered. "I can tell you've already met him."

"I wish I could say that I hadn't but it would be a lie." Maymi'd rather put the memory in the back of her mind and never revisit it again."

"Let me guess what Jensen did to you. He came over here to see you and he demanded that you pack up and move away because your bakery was going to ruin the weight loss of his clients." He laughed.

She didn't find her unpleasant conversation with Casper's brother funny at all. He was insulting and very belittling. She wished she had tossed his ass out sooner than she had done.

"I don't think anything that happened with your brother yesterday was funny," she said, walking around Casper. She guessed rudeness ran in their family.

Today wasn't the time Casper needed to be getting on her bad side. Not with everything she had on her schedule that she needed to get done before leaving work.

"Thank you, Mr. Lowe for your offer but I think I'll pass on it. I don't need your help because this isn't a joke to me. It's my livelihood and I want Sinful to be as successful as it can."

Maymi continued walking to her front door, but stopped when Casper suddenly stepped in her path. "Look, I'm sorry," he apologized. "I wasn't trying to be insensitive about what my brother did to you, but Jensen is always so worried about the big picture that he doesn't take the time to take pleasure in the journey of getting there."

She glared at Casper. "Okay, thanks for telling me but I really don't care about your brother's problems. I've enough of my own to deal with."

"Well, you would have one less if you let me do the boxes. I swear I won't mess the new ones up at all," he promised, holding up two fingers.

A tiny grin pulled at the corners of Maymi's mouth. "I find it hard to believe you were a boy scout," she said, trying not to laugh.

"Oh, I wasn't," Casper admitted, dropping his hand. "But I got you to smile which is even better. I swear to you that I'm not as bad as my big brother. So will you let me help you out or not?"

She might be making a mistake but Casper was just *so* cute that she couldn't turn him down. Besides, what would it hurt if all he wanted to do was put some boxes together for her and he was the reason most of the ones she worked on last night got ruined.

"Okay, I'll let you help me," she finally agreed. "But I better not hear a word about it from your brother. He'll probably die if he knew you were helping the enemy."

"Jensen's problems are his not mine," Casper said, taking the destroyed boxes from her arms. "Come on; let's get this show on the road."

Moving to the side, he got out of the way while she opened the door for him. Maymi watched as Casper carried the boxes through the door. She wondered just how upset Jensen would get over this. He wanted her gone. Yet his brother was over here helping her out.

God, she would love to be a fly on the wall when Casper told Jensen what he spent his morning doing. Without a doubt, the loud screams of Jensen's voice would be echoing through the streets when he found out about this.

"Ms. Monroe, I want to say thank you again for allowing me to do this for you," Casper said, placing the boxes down on the table right in front of them.

"Not a problem. You offered your help and I took it after a little persuasion on your part. I think I was just being stubborn. I knew I needed the help, but I just didn't want to admit to it."

"I can't blame you for turning me down, especially after the way Jensen treated you."

Feeling bad about her earlier attitude, Maymi touched Casper on the arm, giving it a slight squeeze. "You aren't your brother. I shouldn't have judged you like you were. Let me get the other boxes and you can get started putting them together."

Letting go of Casper's arm, she moved away going over to the boxes and wondered where the extra money would come from to replace the other boxes. Money was still very tight. She didn't have a pile of it hidden; however, she wasn't going to allow this small setback to stop her from moving forward.

Chapter Seven

"What smell *so* good?" a male voice asked behind her. "I could smell it all the way out there while I was working on those boxes."

Spinning around, Maymi found Casper standing behind her with a stack of bakery boxes lined up on the table.

"Where did you get those extra boxes?" she questioned, coming up to him. "I know that I didn't give you that many to put together before I came into the kitchen."

"Some of the ones that fell on the ground after our run-in weren't that damaged as we first thought," he told her. "I was able to fix them and they look brand new again. So now are you going to answer my question?"

"I've a couple of pies cooling on the rack. I sold out of them yesterday so I made some more for today. A few customers told me that they would be back today for some more," Maymi answered.

"They look amazing, Casper told her. "You better get ready to sell out again because they will all be gone in a matter of minutes."

She was beginning to like him more and more. He might be a little bit more on the laid back side, but there wasn't anything wrong with that. At least they weren't at each other's throats every time their paths crossed.

"Thank you. I need all of the encouragement I can get," she admitted. Maymi suddenly remembered Casper's deadline and took a glance at the clock on the wall behind him.

"You should be heading to your job. It's almost been an hour. I don't want you to get into any trouble with your brother because of me."

"If Jensen didn't have it in his radar to complain about what I did to ruin his day then he would find something else to lecture me about. It's what makes our relationship run so smoothly.

"However, you're right. I need to go since I need to get set up for my kickboxing class. Good luck with your sales today, but I don't think you will need it," Casper said then smiled at her before walking out the swinging kitchen door.

Hurrying out the door behind Casper, Maymi called out his name and he spun back around. "Thank you again for helping me. I couldn't have made the pies without it," she told him.

"Not a problem. I loved doing it," Casper told her. He waved goodbye before going out her front door and then walking past her bay window.

She wouldn't have made a bet on Jensen's brother running into her this morning and then spending the next hour at her bakery putting boxes together. Her day already started off with a surprise, so she couldn't wait to see where it would go after this. Things only had to be on the up and up; no negative thoughts were even going to enter her mind. They wouldn't do her any good if they did anyway.

Turning away from the window, Maymi headed back to the back to finish boxing up the cupcake order. She had about another forty-five minutes before the customer showed up for them and she wanted to make each second count.

※

"I'm surprised to see you here early. I thought you loved coming in the last minute and making a mad dash to get everything together. What has gotten into you? Did you not stay out last night and party?"

Casper stopped working on one of the boxing gloves and looked up at his brother who was standing next to him.

"Jensen, why are you constantly in such a bad mood? I mean can't you ever say good morning or ask how I'm doing?" he questioned. "I do have feelings and I don't like the way you just seem to forget that sometimes."

Groaning, Jensen ran his fingers through his hair and then sat down on the bench next to him. "Sorry Casper. I've had a hard night and I woke up in a bad mood. I shouldn't have jumped down your throat like I just did. You haven't done anything to me."

"You have too much on your shoulders. I told you that you need to relax more. Get away from the gym and have a little fun. I promise you, it will still be standing when you get back."

Jensen wondered where his brother came up with some of his crazy ideas. Who was going to run the business if he took a break? He had worked *too* hard getting here to let it all go to hell now.

"Like I've told you before, I want to expand the gym, so I need to get that accomplished before I can even think about taking a break. I might have had it done by now, if Ms. Monroe hadn't stolen the building next door from me. I almost had it until she came out of nowhere and snatched it out of my hands."

"Are you seriously still complaining about her," Casper said, tossing the boxing glove down on the floor. "You're giving Maymi too much credit. Besides, I don't think she that's bad. She seems like a very nice person to me."

He turned his head slowly staring at his brother. "How do you know anything about her?" Jensen questioned. "Have you been talking to her or something?"

Casper glanced away from him then a few minutes later made eye contact again. He got a sneaky suspicion that he already knew the answer before his brother said one word.

"Answer me," he demanded.

"Yeah, I literally ran into her this morning and I had a nice conversation with her before I came into work. Man, she's even more gorgeous up close than she is from a distance. In addition, Sinful isn't too bad looking on the inside either. Some of those homemade pies smelled amazing. It reminded me of the ones we used to eat at grandmother's house every Sunday after church."

"Tell me why you went inside of her bakery?" Jensen asked. "I thought you knew to stay away from the competition."

Jumping up from the bench, Casper shook his head at him. "Jensen, Maymi isn't your competition. Her bakery has nothing to do with Fitness 24 and you know that she isn't the reason you didn't get the building either. Two different businesses can be right next door and work together without any issues. She told me that you came to see her and from her tone I can tell that things didn't end well between the two of you."

Jensen took a quick sharp breath so he wouldn't yell at Casper. He didn't want to put anymore tension between them. "I think it would be for the best if we both stayed away from Ms. Monroe. I don't want any more animosity than there already is between us."

Picking up the gloves off the floor, Casper stood up and looked down at him. "She only has a problem with you. We got along pretty good this morning at her bakery. So, maybe you're the one who needs to stay away from her," his brother said before stalking away.

He jumped up from the bench and started to follow after his brother but stopped when he spotted some members coming into class. Now wasn't the time to continue this conversation, he would get into it later on after work. They weren't done and he hoped that Casper didn't think they were.

Walking to the door, he took one last look over his shoulder, pleased to see Casper at least interacting with everyone inside the room instead of only the pretty women. Casper might actually be listening to his advice more than he thought; however, only time would tell with his younger sibling.

Jensen took one final glance before going out the door and he was on his way back upstairs to his office when he caught a figure from the corner of his eye standing at the front desk.

What in the world was she doing inside his gym? Had she lost her mind or was she trying to push his buttons?

He never told her that she couldn't step foot in here, but why would she want to when she knew where they stood with each other? He had drawn a line in the sand and she purposely crossed it to send his blood pressure up another notch.

Storming towards Maymi, Jensen didn't stop until he was standing right next to her. He glanced down at the two boxes in her hand hoping she hadn't brought any of her desserts inside of his business.

"Krissy, what's going on here?" he asked his receptionist then looked back at Maymi who was glaring at him. "Is she trying to sell you some of her fattening foods?"

"Jensen, this lady wanted to leave something for Casper, but I told her you didn't allow desserts inside the gym," Krissy answered, glancing away from Maymi over to him.

"I'm not trying to cause any problems. All I wanted to do was leave a thank you gift for Casper. He helped me out this morning and then had to leave before the pies and cupcakes were done."

"Ms. Monroe, my receptionist told you correctly. I think you should take your sweets and leave. I'll tell my brother about them after he has finished with his classes. If Casper wants them, he can come over to your bakery and pick them up there."

Why did she always have to draw his attention with her fresh yet tempting looks?

He tried not to notice how attractive Maymi looked in her black apron with *Sinful* written across the top in hot pink. Casper wasn't lying about her being a good-looking woman; it was just too bad they both were on opposite ends.

"You can't be serious about not taking these," she questioned, shoving the delicious smelling boxes underneath his nose making him get another whiff of cinnamon and apples.

"Yes, I'm very serious," Jensen answered, moving the boxes away from his face. "If you're looking for a taster of your treats, you came to the wrong place. No one here wants any piece of any of your over-iced cupcakes."

Chocolate eyes narrowed at him before Maymi laid the boxes on the desk in front of Krissy. She was still standing there watching the argument between them with an amused look on her face.

Jensen didn't back down, but took a step closer to her curvy body. If she wanted to fight then a fight is what she would get. He wasn't about to back down from a five feet something pastry chef.

"How dare you insult my grandmother's cupcakes," she hissed. "I would never over-ice them. My red velvet cupcakes are even better than my pecan pie. Don't talk about something you know nothing about, Mr. Lowe."

"I wasn't insulting your grandmother. I was talking about you, princess."

Maymi stopped talking and just stared at him with a vacant look in her eyes. Now, what was her problem with him? She was looking at him like she couldn't believe he just called her that.

"Don't call me princess," she said in a low voice.

"Why not?" he asked. "You're acting like a spoiled little princess."

"I won't tell you again not to call me that name."

He thought he saw her eyes grow a little sadder, but Maymi blinked and then turned away so he couldn't be sure if he hadn't imagined the entire thing or not.

"Don't forget to give those treats to Casper as soon as his class ends. I'll know if you tossed them in the trash and I'll be back over to get you if you do it."

Jensen stood next to the desk and watched in utter disbelief as Maymi ignored his comment and continued on out the front door like she hadn't heard him talking to her. Why did he ever bother dealing with that woman?

"Can you believe she did that to me?" He spun back around in time to catch Krissy biting into one of the red velvet cupcakes Maymi had left for his brother.

"What are you doing?" Had everyone just lost their minds since Sinful moved next door or was Krissy trying to make him fire her on the spot.

"Sorry boss," she mumbled around the treat in her mouth. "I love red velvet cupcakes and these are outstanding. I swear you need to try one and you will change your mind about Ms. Monroe. She has a true gift. After tasting one, I'm going to buy some and take them to my son's class tomorrow for his teacher's retirement party."

"No, thank you." He closed the cupcake box and grabbed it along with the other one off the counter. "When Casper finishes with his last class tell him that I need to see him in my office."

Jensen could already see where this was going and it wouldn't be good for their bottom dollar. He was going to tell Casper he didn't need to see or talk to her anymore

"I sure will," Krissy said before taking another huge bit out of the fluffy cupcake and moaning softly.

Swallowing down his criticism, Jensen turned away from the reception desk and made his way towards the staircase leading upstairs to his office. How was he supposed to get Maymi away from next door if Casper was trying to befriend her just to spite him?

God, it was days like this than he wished he was an only child!

Chapter Eight

Pausing in front of the trash can by the side of his desk, Jensen thought about tossing Maymi's gifts for his brother right on inside, but stopped himself at the very last minute. They weren't his to toss. He would keep his word and give them to Casper when he came to see him.

Going across the room, Jensen laid the two boxes down on a table where he usually ate his lunch. Today wasn't the day he wanted to run into Maymi again. Normally, he tried to avoid confrontations whenever it was possible, but something about her pushed him to do battle with her anytime they were within five feet of each other.

*It is desire...*his mind snickered. *You want her. Stop denying it.* He shook his head getting rid of the nonsense floating around up there.

Working and running Fitness 24 was more important to him that it seemed to be to his brother and ex-girlfriend. Most of his friends had found ways to avoid him so they wouldn't get caught up in listening to his ideas for this place, but he couldn't help it.

He was continually trying to live up to his potential and achieve recognition as the top gym owner in town. Nothing was going to stand in his way of getting that item crossed off his list before moving on to the next one.

Was it really wrong for him to be confident in his abilities to make it happen? Carrying out all of his projects with purpose and passion is what made him jump up out of bed every morning.

Fitness 24 was his life.

He had worked too many odd jobs over the years to make this place a reality. He wasn't about to lose his dream now because of 'Little Miss Bakery'.

Unquestionably, she had to be the most difficult and trying

woman he had ever run across. Even during the five years he spent as a male stripper to save up money to start this place, none of those women in the night clubs had gotten under his skin the way Maymi did.

She *loved* pulling his strings. He saw the pleasure in her eyes earlier when she stood there holding her boxes of devilish treats. She purposely came over there to rub him the wrong way and not to see Casper. She was getting him back for when he barged into her business and made all of those demands.

However, he doubted Maymi hadn't counted on her visit only fueling his fire even more. He had a very difficult time not picking up her enticing body and carrying her right back out the front door. She wasn't ready to deal with that tougher side of him.

So he allowed her to believe that she had won this round, but he always had something else up his sleeve. When the right time presented itself, he would show her.

As much as he wanted to keep his mind focused on his dealings with Maymi, Jensen had to get more done on the new projects he had on his outline. Fitness 24 still wasn't the premier gym he knew it could be. Everything he had written down on paper had worked out amazingly, but only a few things were left to get accomplished and time was running out to get them done.

Glancing down at his wrist, he noticed his watch showed he only had a few minutes to leave and head over to his appointment with Jack Metz. He was surprised to find a message on his phone from his toughest competition in town.

Everyone around town had heard the rumors blowing around town that Jack was interested in selling his privately owned establishment. His curiosity was piqued by why his nemesis wanted to sell his grandfather's business to him.

Were the rumors he heard actually true about the high-end workout center? Could Jack's members be leaving because of the lack of professionalism shown their by his trainers? Could they really be hitting on their female clients and nothing had happened to the guys?

If Jack had allowed all of this to happen and turned a blind eye to keep his employees then he needed to lose his reputation and his business along with it. He didn't and wouldn't tolerate any of his trainers, employees male or female, to disrespect anyone before or during their workout sessions.

Turning around, he hurried for the door knowing that Jack might not like the price he wanted to offer him, but it would be a good offer since Health Pro, Inc. wasn't up to the standards it use to have for people previously. A bad name attached to a building for a year and a half, it was going to take time to rebuild it back up but he could do it for the right price along with the help of Casper.

Finally being able to give Casper a place of his own would give him the opportunity to make his sibling prove himself. It was a great opportunity to show him that he could run the huge kickboxing classes he kept bragging about.

For months now, he had been complaining about wanting a bigger space to expand his classes to include more than fifteen people. Health Pro, Inc. was a lot smaller than Fitness 24 in some ways, but there was one huge spot that could be perfect for what Casper was craving to do with his talent.

He prayed everything would run smoothly with Jack and he could be signing the paperwork in the next few weeks. Maybe having something else to give his attention to would get Casper's mind off of the pretty Maymi.

Opening his office door, Jensen stepped out then stumbled back to avoid running into his brother standing on the other side. "Shit, I almost ran right into you."

Casper held up his hands and took his own step back. "Sorry, I didn't know you were about to leave." He apologized, dropping his hands. "Krissy told me that Maymi dropped off two delicious thank you gifts for me and that you had brought them up here."

"Yes, she did. They're over there on the table by the window," Jensen said, pointing a finger over his shoulder. "I'm running late to see Jack Metz. So we'll have to talk about her visit later on when I get the time."

"I know you won't forget," Casper mumbled under his breath but he still heard him.

"Of course I won't." Jensen brushed past his brother and continued down the hallway towards the staircase.

He was running late, so he had to make it worth Jack's time to wait for him. Health Pro. Inc, was almost in the palm of his hand and he wasn't about to have it snatched away for no good reason.

Chapter Nine

"Come on and tell me what has put that horrible look on your face," Jazmaine complained, waving a potato chip in her face.

Twenty minutes ago, Jazmaine surprised her with her favorite Subway sandwich for lunch. She was even nice enough to eat in the back of the bakery while she worked on patty cakes and then cookies. Now she was acting like a first class bitch by not answering her questions.

Honestly, food was the last thing on her mind until Jazmaine showed up with sandwiches and that friendly smile of hers she loved so much. After eating several bites, Maymi had to admit her headache was better and she could think a lot clearer than before. "I had a run-in with Jensen again," Maymi finally answered, dropping her food down on the Subway paper in front of her. "I swear that man must wake up on the wrong side of the bed every single morning. He never has a kind word for anyone."

"Tell me what happened this time. Did he come back over here again and throw another tantrum demanding you move away from him or else?"

Shaking her head, Maymi pushed a potato around with her finger. "No, this time I was at Fitness 24. He just happened to see me and he threw a major fit. I thought he was literally going to pick me up and toss me out on the sidewalk," she admitted.

She tried glancing away from her friend, but Jazmaine's eyes caught and held hers. "Sweetie, I think you and Jensen just need to stay away from each other as much as possible. Why you decided to make an appearance at his gym, I will never know. Usually, you are so reasonable and practical when dealing with people. So why does he seem to get underneath your skin so badly?"

"I believe our personalities clashed so hard the first time because I made a decision then not to let him intimidate me again.

"Jensen seems to believe that he is the only one who has worked their ass off to make their business where it is today. Well, he hasn't and I'm still angry he came over here and got in my face almost telling me I was too worthless to handle running this place.

"I won't let him, or anyone else, take this away from me. I've worked too hard to get this far. My pastry arts degree means the world to me and it will help me attain a profitable business doing something I love."

"Oh, I see what the problem is now. It has become a lot clearer to me," Jazmaine told her.

"I don't know what you're talking about," Maymi said. She started clearing away the trash off the table leftover from her lunch.

"Has your father called you at all since the grand opening? I know you called and told him about it; despite the fact, he hasn't been all of that supportive of your career choice."

Getting up from her seat, she tossed the remains of her sandwich into her trashcan. Why did Jazmaine have to bring up her father? She wasn't in the mood to discuss her father.

"Maymi, are you going to answer me?" her girlfriend asked from right behind her.

She spun around and took Jazmaine's trash from her. "No, I haven't heard from him, but you know that he isn't big on giving words of encouragement to the only girl in the family."

"I can't believe your father treats you so differently from your brothers. Surely, he's still not mad because you decided to go after you own dream and not the one he had picked out for you."

She understood that Jazmaine was trying to be a good friend to her, but this conversation was going nowhere. They had been talking about Jensen and somehow it had turned down a side street and gotten onto her father.

"Look, I know—"

The beeping sound of the timer cut Maymi off signaling to her that it was time to take the cookies out of the oven. Walking away from her girlfriend, she grabbed a potholder off the counter then went over to the oven and removed the cookies. Maymi moved around Jazmaine and sat the cookie sheet down before she worked on removing the warm cookies to a rack.

"Maymi, you need to talk about this. I know you're upset with your dad, but you need to fix things with him."

"Aren't you going to be late getting back to work?" she asked, hoping Jazmaine took the blatant hint and left it alone.

"Alright, I got it. You want me to leave but I do have one more thing to tell you. You aren't going anywhere and I doubt Jensen is going to uproot his gym to a new location either. So the two of you need to get along or find a better way to avoid each other."

Angry at the advice which came across more like an attack on her, Maymi twirled around giving Jazmaine a look. "Why do I have to be the one getting a lecture? He started the feud with me. I was minding my own business working away and he came over to my bakery…it wasn't the other way around. I only went over to Fitness 24 so I could see Casper. I had no interest in looking at his face or hearing his voice for that matter."

"I'm not giving you a lecture. I'm only pointing out the facts. The more you stay away from him the more productive your day will go." Jazmaine looked her directly in the eye. "If you see him coming go the other way, it will keep down the arguments. You want to use all of that energy to draw more customers through the doors. Fitness 24 had been around a while and already has a name in the community. Sinful has only been here months. You can't let him detour you anymore than he already has."

"I—"

"Honey, just try it my way for a few days and see how it works out for you. Ignore anything he might toss your way and direct those emotions towards a different goal. Didn't you mention you need to design some extra promotional materials for the bakery? Have you given any more thought to getting a website up and running?"

Maymi knew Jazmaine was right and admitting it was a little painful but she couldn't lie. "Yes, I'm running the idea through my head, but I've been working on this life-sized customized Hello Kitty cake that I'm getting close to ten thousand dollars for. I mean it's my first huge order for Sinful. I just can't get into getting a website set up right now."

Jazmaine grinned at her. "See, that is what I'm talking about, focusing your attention on your gifts and not some guy who came out of nowhere to be a thorn in your side. I know you're feisty and don't back down from a battle, but just take a step back from Jensen. Unless there's another reason you like the tension brewing between the two of you."

The memory of how she used to be burned in her mind. Jazmaine was right. She had lost some of that woman and the thought of becoming her again was exciting.

"I'll see what I can do about getting the old me back, but I need to finish baking and taking things out of the oven before my help comes back here screaming for more sweets I don't have."

"Don't you have anything else to say to me?"

"Like what," she said, walking up to Jazmaine.

"Maybe you're sexually attracted to Jensen and that is one of the motivations for arguing with him. I mean I can't blame you if it's true. Who wouldn't want the guy? He oozes that let's have a one night stand kind of allure about him."

Laughing, Maymi hugged her crazy friend. She always thought it was Tatum she had to be worried about because of her crazy ideas, but now Jazmaine was giving her a run for her money with that comment.

"No, I don't see him as a sexy one night stand. Isn't the purpose of a one night stand to sleep with the hot stranger and never see him again? Jensen is right next door to me, so that wouldn't work for me. Not that I was thinking about doing it," she quickly added. "But thanks again for coming to see me. Our talk really helped me a lot, I see things more differently now than before."

"Honey, after the way you left the restaurant two weeks ago I had no choice but to come and see about you as soon as I could. Listen I know I'm busy with the Mashiro deal, but if you need help with anything let me know and I'll make the time for you."

Spinning around, Jazmaine grabbed her purse off the table and walked over to the kitchen door as the second buzzer went off for the cupcakes behind Maymi. She gave her friend one more look before going over to the oven and taking out her double chocolate treats. The mint frosting was already done and waiting at the side for the cupcakes once they were cool enough to ice.

As she removed the cupcakes out of the oven, Maymi couldn't get Jazmaine's words out of her head. She was here to stay for the long haul and he better get used to it. Sinful was hers after years of working hard and nothing Jensen threatened her with was going to frighten her away.

Chapter Ten

"Ms. Monroe, are you sure that you don't need me to stay here with you? It already eight-thirty and it's pretty dark outside."

Glancing up from the dinosaur cake she was working on, Maymi spotted her assistant Olivia standing in the open doorway of the kitchen. She thought Olivia had already left and gone home for the night.

"No, I'm fine. You can go ahead and leave to pick your daughter up from dance practice. I only need to finish up a few more things on him then I'm out of here too. How does the case look out there?"

"It looks really good. You're out of fresh pies and those little chocolate cream filled snacks," Olivia answered.

"Great, thanks for reminding me about those. I'll work on them tomorrow morning when I get here at six o'clock."

"Are you sure about me leaving? I know it's a pretty safe neighborhood, but you did park across the street near the basketball court because it was street cleaning day. I don't feel right leaving you here alone. I can call my husband and he can pick up Meagan instead of me."

Wiping her hands on the towel, Maymi came around the counter and stopped in front of Olivia. She was touched her assistant was concerned about her safety, but there wasn't any need for her to be.

"I'll be perfectly safe. This won't be the first time I left Sinful at night and it won't be the last time I do it either. Now, get out of here and pick up your little girl. Remember, I need you to come in at ten o'clock tomorrow. I have to finish up this dinosaur cake along with the hundred count cupcake order."

"Have you thought about hiring a few more people to help you out?" Olivia asked. "I know my sister- in-law is an amazing cake decorator and she was looking for part-time work."

"Right now, I don't have the extra money so I can't do it. Besides, I've a good system that keeps things easy for me. However, if I start getting more customized cakes orders, I will have to hire two more people. Now, enough worrying about me. You can't have your daughter waiting for you at the dance studio."

"Okay, if you're sure," Olivia hedged. "I just don't feel right leaving you here to walk across the street alone while my car is parked right out front."

"Don't, I should have moved mine back after they finished cleaning the street, but I didn't do it. Besides, I'm pretty sure nothing is going to happen to me. I'm honestly not scared to walk the short distance to my car."

Olivia gave her another doubtful look before spinning around and walking away. Maymi followed behind her and waited while her assistant got her things, so she could lock up and turn over the sign on the front door to closed.

She would be out of here early for once on a Friday night. She might even stay up late and read for an hour or two which was something she hadn't done in a while.

"I want you to be safe and check everything before you leave," Olivia told her, heading for the exit.

"Okay, Mom. I'll do that," she teased, standing at the door watching as Olivia got inside of her vehicle, waved at her then drove off.

She closed the door, locked it and then turned over the sign before spinning around and hurrying back to the kitchen. She wanted to keep up with the time so she could out of here exactly on time for once.

Today's sales turned out to be more profitable than she thought after the slower than usual start. If every day became a regular day with a steady flow of customers, she would be able to hire two more assistants in the back and another one to work up the front with Olivia.

Humming to herself, Maymi went back through the door and sat back down on her stool. She picked up the carving tool and began working on the fine details on the mouth and eyes for the dinosaur.

When she first took the order and the boy's father had told her what he wanted done, she turned him down until he offered to pay extra for the background on the cake. Every extra dollar earned went right back into Sinful, so she agreed to have it ready for him by late Saturday afternoon.

Good thing she didn't open up until ten o'clock on Saturdays. She could come in and have the entire place to herself for hours until Olivia showed up to open the doors.

Maymi continued working on the tiny details on the nose, mouth and teeth until everything looked exactly like the picture on the table given to her by the customer. She laid down the tool then glanced up at the clock. She had the last part of the cake with an extra ten minutes to spare. All she had to do tomorrow was add the last of the finishing touches and the little guy would be ready to pick up.

Picking up the dinosaur, Maymi took it over to the cooler, placed it inside making sure to block the door so it wouldn't slam closed and lock her on the inside since it had been acting crazy for the past couple of days.

She had been meaning to call someone to check on it, but with not having the extra money she was dealing with it the best way she could and nothing had gone wrong so far. Leaving the ice box, she made her way back over to her work area and she spent the next ten minutes cleaning up her tools then wiped off the counter.

She folded the rag and laid it across the sink as she took one final look around her work space. Every piece of equipment was in the correct spot before leaving the kitchen so she could finally go home and get lost inside the new mystery book she bought at the mall a week ago. Walking through the bakery, she stopped at the wall long enough to flick off the lights before going outside.

The warm night air brushed against her bare arms while she locked the front door. Maymi spun around and just as she was about to walk across the street a loud sound of voices coming from around the side of her bakery caught her attention.

"Listen asshole. We aren't about to tell you again. Do as we tell you and you won't get hurt," a man's angry voice snapped.

Easing closer to the side of the building, she stood there wondering if she should peek around the corner to see what was going on or hurry to her car instead and speed off leaving whoever might need her help alone.

"I'm not giving you a damn thing," a voice she immediately recognized hollered.

Jensen. She would know his cocky voice anywhere.

"Why don't we give this pretty boy a lesson in manners?"

Maymi heard someone snicker before the sound of fist hitting bone sounded out around her and then Jensen's deep, rich voice screaming out in pain. She started to take a look then stopped herself. She needed a plan before she just jumped into something she didn't know anything about.

"Hit him again. Kick him harder. Show this cocky asshole what happens when guys like him don't give us what we want," another guy yelled as Jensen hollered out in agony again.

Digging into her purse, Maymi grabbed her cell phone before going around the corner. She gasped at the sight of a battered and bruised Jensen lying on the ground bleeding by the side of his white truck.

"Leave him alone," she screamed, making the two guy jump away from his prone body. "I've called the cops and they are on the way."

God, she hoped they believe her bluff because her cell phone battery died on the way to work this morning and she had forgotten to charge it. She didn't know what else she could do if they decided to test her.

"Hey, look here. The little bakery lady is trying to get tough." A tall red haired guy laughed and moved towards her. "I don't believe you called anyone pretty lady. You're just trying to scare us. I'm pretty sure I can take you. I mean you aren't that big."

"Leave her alone," Jensen yelled behind her before the guy standing next to him kicked him in the ribs. "She has nothing to do with any of this."

"Are you sure?" Maymi bluffed as her heart pounded away inside of her chest.

Why had she even opened her mouth or showed her face? It wasn't like Jensen was her favorite person in the world to begin with. She could have walked away, gotten inside of her car and driven away and no one would have been the wiser.

Because you are a good person and you would have remembered leaving someone screaming out in pain, her mind whispered, softly.

"I'm positive, pretty lady," the guy said coming even closer as the sound of police sirens suddenly echoed in the distance out of nowhere.

"Fuck!"

Maymi tried to keep the surprise off her face as he took a step back from her. "See, I told you I had called the police. You better get out of here before they get here and arrest your sorry asses."

"Hell, I'm out of here. I'm not about to go back to jail. I'm already on probation," the younger guy said, standing next to Jensen. He spun around and ran back towards the car parked at the far end of Fitness 24 near some trees.

"Aren't you going to follow your buddy?" she asked, staring at the other man.

"I won't forget this, bitch," he warned her. "You'll get yours." He glared at her for only a few more seconds before taking off after his friend.

Slowly, some of her fear eased away as he hopped into the car at the corner and it took off in the opposite direction of the sirens. Holding the phone against her chest, she took several deep breaths as her heart continued to pound away against her ribs.

She sent up a silent prayer of thanks to whoever called the cops just at the right time. They weren't coming here, but it was enough to scare those two thugs into running away leaving her alone to give Jensen some help.

Tossing her cell phone back into her purse, Maymi rushed over to Jensen who was holding his side struggling to get up off the pavement as blood slid from the corner of his mouth.

"Here, let me help you," she said, wrapping her arm around his waist.

"No, I got it," Jensen, said, his dark brown eyes clashing with hers.

She tried not to stare at how beautiful they looked up close with their faces only being inches apart. He might get on her last nerve, but he was *fine* as hell and the sad thing was he knew it too.

"Well, it's a good thing you do because I'm going to need your help getting you back to the bakery," she told him, blowing off the glare he was giving her.

"No, you can help me back to my business," Jensen told her as he started leaning some of his weight on her as he slowly stood up. "I'll call Casper from there to help me."

"No, Sinful is closer and you can call your brother after we call the cops. Now, will you stop fighting with me so I can get you there? You aren't the lightest man in the world."

Jensen's eyes flashed for a second like he was going to get all macho on her, but he only shook his head and wrapped his arm around her shoulder. She tried to move as fast as she could with his muscular frame leaning against her.

Despite the fact, he was beat up, bloody and his clothing was tattered, the scent of his cologne was making her very aware of him as a man.

What was wrong with her body? How could it be drawn to someone like Jensen?

This guy hated her and wanted her off his block like tomorrow, but here she was helping him to the place he hated more than anything in the world. She might be too kind-hearted for her own good or something was truly mentally wrong with her.

"Can you stand while I unlock the door for us?" she asked, moving his arm off her shoulder.

"Yeah, I think so," Jensen hissed, holding his side. "Damn, those SOB's really did a number on me. I think they might have bruised some of my ribs."

Maymi quickly snatched her keys out of her purse, unlocked the door and helped Jensen inside and sat him down in a chair next to the display case.

"God, let me get something to clean up your face," she said, touching his jaw.

Jensen touched her hand and the warmth of his calloused fingers made her panties instantly wet. "No, I'm fine. All I need is something to drink and I'll get out of your hair. I can call the cops and Casper from my house."

Men. Why did they always try to pretend nothing was wrong when everything was?

"I don't think so. I'm going to grab the first aid kit out of the kitchen. You can get in touch with your brother and law enforcement while I'm gone," she said, walking over to the cordless phone by the cash register. She picked it up and brought it back over to Jensen.

"Here, I'll bring you something back to drink too."

Jensen stared at the phone for a few minutes before taking it from her. She didn't feel like she needed to stay to make sure he actually made the phone calls. She turned away and went the short distance into the kitchen.

Once Maymi was alone she held out her hands and noticed how badly they were shaking. Shit! She could have gotten herself hurt or Jensen beaten up more than he already was if those police sirens hadn't saved her lying ass at exactly the perfect moment.

Who in the hell were those guys and why were they beating up Jensen? Sure, she had dreamt about punching him since their first disastrous encounter, but she wouldn't really do it no matter how far he pushed her.

The dull ache of fear still clung to her body at the memories of the guy's hate filled eyes as he stared at her. His face might be burned into her mind for a while, if she let it, but she wouldn't allow him to have the kind of power over her.

Yet, the warmth of Jensen's body brushing against hers would still be with her after she went to bed tonight alone. He was bothering her in so many ways. Some of them were good of course, some of them weren't. She hated to admit he left a burning imprint on her body anytime he was around her.

Damn him for being so good-looking!

Pushing her body away from the door, Maymi got everything she needed from the kitchen and then headed back to the front of the bakery. She walked in on Jensen, catching the tail end of his conversation.

"Casper, I'm fine. No, I don't have a head injury," Jensen shouted. "You did hear me correctly when I told you to pick me up at Sinful. Yes, Maymi really helped me and brought me over here. Alright, I promise I won't be an asshole before you show up. Just get your ass over here." He pushed the end button and then his eyes suddenly darted over in her direction.

"I guess you heard that," he said.

"Yes, I did," Maymi answered. She walked up to Jensen and handed him the bottled water. She waited while he undid the lid and took a long swallow before sitting it down next to him on the table.

"I guess Casper couldn't believe I lifted a finger to help you after the way you've been treating me," she said, placing the first aid kit down on the table.

"He thought I'd gotten hit too hard in the head. It took me a minute to make him believe what I was telling him was the truth," Jensen admitted.

Opening it, she took out a few things so she could get started cleaning up his cuts and wounds. She hadn't done anything like this since her last boyfriend took a tumble off his motorcycle.

Hudson had loved that bike so much that he didn't even think about wearing a helmet. No matter how much she pushed for him to do it, he constantly told her no and if he had only listened to her that one day... Maymi quickly shook the thought from her head when Jensen's voice caught her attention.

"What did you say?" she asked dipping the cotton ball into the small alcohol container.

"I asked if you were okay," he said, staring at her. "You had this faraway look in your eyes. Are you still thinking about those two guys?"

"No," Maymi answered. Honestly, the attackers from earlier were the last two people on her mind. Taking the cotton ball, she touched it to the small cut on Jensen's forehead. She doubted the scratch would even leave a scar, so he would still be as handsome as ever.

"Fuck," he cursed, moving back from her. "That shit stinks. Are you trying to cause me more pain on purpose?"

"Of course not," she uttered, placing the cotton ball there again and this time Jensen didn't move.

Maymi continued working on getting what cuts and bruises she could get cleaned out while ignoring how intensely Jensen was watching her. She was so close to him that she could feel his breath brushing against her face.

Her senses were spun by the scent of him; the warmth of his soft flesh was intoxicating. She was fully aware of the hardness of his thighs brushing over her legs. The old saying there was a thin line between love and hate was a lie because right now she was having a hard time with the thin line between lust and hate. There was no way she was in love with Jensen, but her *lust* for him was off the scales.

"Hey," Jensen said, touching her hand. He moved it from the side of his face.

"What?" she asked, blinking before looking at him directly in the eyes. She removed her hand from his light grasp and her skin tingled from the heat of his touch.

"Why did you help me? I haven't been the nicest guy to you.

You could have left me out there and it might have been hours before anyone found me back there."

She felt his breath on her cheek as he studied her waiting for an answer from her. "I thought about it, but I'm not that kind of person. I would have been thinking about what happened to you all night. No matter how badly we don't get along or hate each other, I wouldn't leave my worst enemy or even you lying out there alone in pain. It wouldn't sit well on my conscience," she said, turning way and starting to clean up the mess next to her.

"Thank you," Jensen said, touching her on the arm.

Maymi glanced down at Jensen's long, tanned fingers before moving away. "You're welcome," she said, just as someone knocked on the door.

Turning, she saw two police officers standing there. She didn't even remember locking the door, but she could have done it in the frenzy of everything that had been going on. Going over to it, she unlocked it and moved back so they could come inside.

"Ma'am, we got a call about someone getting attacked," the older officer said to her.

"Yes, it was Mr. Lowe," she said, pointing over to Jensen. She watched as the officer left her and walked over to him, leaving her alone with the second younger and cuter officer.

"Did you witness this assault as well?" he asked her.

"Yes, I saw the end of the attack." Maymi wondered how much of this she would be dragged into. It was getting late and she needed to get home because she had to be back here so early.

"I need to get your statement as well," the officer informed her.

"Okay."

"It should only take a few minutes and then you can be on your way."

After answering several questions and giving a description of both men, the cops finally left twenty minutes later. Once they were gone, Maymi finished cleaning up everything while Jensen drank the cup of coffee she fixed for him while still waiting for Casper to show up.

"I swear my brother doesn't know how to be punctual if it bit him on the ass," Jensen complained, sitting his hot coffee cup down on the table. "I know you hate spending all of this extra time with me."

"You're making too much out of it," Maymi replied. She really didn't mind Jensen begin this close to her. "It hasn't been that long since you called him and I'm sure Casper is on his way. You can stay here while you wait for him. I'll be back after I throw all of this into the trash."

Leaving the room, she prayed Casper showed up because she didn't know how much longer she could handle being around Jensen and seeing this side of his personality. He was acting differently towards her, but she wasn't taking it seriously. He would be back to his nasty and sarcastic self tomorrow.

He was the man who hated her, so why was she feeling the tiniest bit sorry for him?

Chapter Eleven

Reaching for the cup of coffee Maymi had fixed for him, Jensen watched her as she left him to go back into the other room. He couldn't help but notice the way her jeans hugged her full ass. He had always been a butt man and hers was near perfect. It was such a shame they were on different ends of the scale, because she was a gorgeous looking female. He wouldn't mind asking her out on a date.

However, he wouldn't ever let that happen because Maymi didn't know how to listen. He wasn't asking a lot of her but she acted like her world was over if she found a new location for her bakery of devilish treats. Tonight, she might have gone out of her way to help him but he seriously doubted if the two of them would ever be friends...or lovers.

His slight attraction to her luscious body would go away, it only occurred because they had been so close to each other while she worked on fixing up his cuts. Maymi never noticed how his gaze was riveted on her face then moved over her body, slowly coming to stop at the deep opening in her hot pink t-shirt.

Most of the time, he never took a second glance at a woman with curves, but Maymi's body was perfectly proportioned in all of the right places. He would be crazy not to find her attractive, but he wouldn't be sidetracked by a pretty face and seductive body.

"You do know if you are planning something against Maymi, it will come to bite you in the ass?"

Turning his head, Jensen found Casper standing not five feet from him. *Was he so lost in thought that he didn't hear the bell chime?*

"How long have you been standing there?"

"Long enough to know that look on your face, your mind was working overtime which is never a good thing. Care to share your thoughts, big brother?"

"Yeah, why are you so late?" he demanded, placing his cup down on the table. He stood up wincing as a pain shot through his left side. He was beginning to rethink turning down medical treatment because he didn't have any broken ribs, but they were killing the hell out of him now.

"Man, I live way across town and there was an accident. So the cops had two of the streets blocked off. I couldn't go the way I usually do. How about a thank you for showing up here to pick up your ungrateful ass; besides, why aren't you driving your truck home instead of demanding I come to pick you up?"

"One of the guys flattened the tires," Jensen answered. "I think they were the two guys I tossed out of Fitness 24 last week for harassing two female members."

"I remember them," his brother said. "They were a piece of work. The red headed one did promise to come back and kick your ass. I guess he kept his word."

Enough already! He was tired of the shit!

"Can't we just—"

"Casper, I didn't know you were out here," Maymi's soft voice said as she walked right past him over to his brother.

"If I could have backed out of picking up Mr. Ungrateful, I would have done it but no one else wants to deal with him," Casper said, smiling at Maymi. "I need to thank you for the treats. I ate a piece of the pie and it was delicious. I'm going to need to run an extra mile in the morning to work it off."

"As long as you don't collide with any more innocent bakery owners, I think you should be fine," she teased back.

Jealousy ate at Jensen while he watched the scene play out in front of him. Both Maymi and his brother teased around each other like he wasn't even in the room. How did they become so friendly with each other after only one meeting?

Well, Casper could flirt with Maymi on his own time and that wasn't tonight! He called him here to pick him up and not to find a way to get Maymi out on a date. His body was craving a hot shower, and a stiff drink before he went to bed and neither one would happen if he stayed here staring at this nonsense.

"Casper, are you ready to go?" he demanded roughly. "I need

to get home."

Pivoting, Maymi stared at him with confusion on her face while his brother shot him a disbelieving look above her head. Shit! He hadn't meant to sound so rude, but his body was killing him.

No...it's your surprise jealousy that has you acting like a bear with a thorn in his paw.

"Casper, your brother is right. You should get him home. As fast as possible, I mean if he spends another moment in my bakery he might break out in hives and we couldn't have that, could we?" she said, looking in his direction not his brother's.

"Fine, we can go. Grab your stuff, Maymi, and you can walk out with us. I'm not going to leave you here alone."

Dragging her eyes way from him, she glanced at Casper. "Thank you. All I need to do is grab my purse and I'm ready to go." Maymi walked back across the room and picked it up off the table where he was still standing beside the chair.

"Well, come on Mr. Lowe. I don't want to keep you from getting your beauty sleep. I can only imagine how someone like you loves getting his full eight hours of sleep."

He took a step into her personal space. Jensen watched how Maymi's big brown bedroom eyes widened in surprise. He lowered his voice, so only she could hear him.

"You like pushing me, Ms. Monroe. Keep it up and see what happens when I decide to give it back to you. I'm not my brother. I don't find a way to turn everything into a joke."

"Oh, I know you aren't Casper. He's the nice one and you're not," Maymi tossed back before spinning away and going over to his brother.

Jensen had seen Casper with a lot of women but for some reason he didn't like how fast he found a way to make Maymi like him. He wasn't fond of it at all. Jensen continued watching the two of them as he walked behind them as his brother opened the door for Maymi then went out behind her.

Impatiently, he stood outside next to Casper's sports car waiting while his brother told her goodbye at her car and then actually waited until she drove off before jogging back over to him.

Where in the hell had that chivalrous quality come from with him?

He wasn't used to seeing his baby brother caring about anyone but himself. For some reason, seeing him be concerned enough to do something like that for Maymi angered him.

"You need to stay away from her," Jensen warned Casper right before he got into the car.

"Are you jealous she likes me better than you?" he asked, getting inside the car and closing the door.

"Of course not," he answered just a little too quickly hating how Casper smirked at him.

"So why are you acting like you are?" Casper questioned before tearing away from the curb in his Mustang.

I'm not jealous. I could care less about the two of them doing anything together. Keep lying to yourself, his mind taunted.

His baby brother was a ladies' man and maybe Maymi was just too naïve or dumb to see it, but she better smarten up or she would end up in the graveyard of failed relationships that seemed to follow Casper everywhere he went.

CHAPTER TWELVE

Standing in front of his bedroom window, Jensen took a sip of his beer as he looked out over his property. Casper had left him about an hour ago to do God knows what for the rest of the night to only show up late for work tomorrow morning.

At first, he only had to worry about Casper flirting with the females at Fitness 24; however, now his brother had a pretty distraction not a hundred feet away from their job. Maymi would keep him so unfocused if he allowed it to happen, but he wouldn't do it.

Yet tonight she really surprised him by stepping up to help him against the two men attacking him. She didn't back down or show an ounce of fear. She showed him a different side of her tonight and he was impressed by it.

A tinge of guilt suddenly hit him. He shouldn't have left the bakery without telling Maymi thanks again for helping him out, but he was beyond ready to leave when Casper showed up with his practiced smile and smooth words. Besides, he wouldn't want Maymi to think they were becoming friends or anything.

She had helped him out of a difficult situation but neither one of them have forgotten why they would always be at odds. She had something he wanted…and Maymi wasn't about to give it up.

Walking away from the window, Jensen went back over to his bed and got in, resting his back against two pillows hoping to ease some of the ache in his side. His ribs still hurt, but not as badly as earlier. Wrapping them up helped out a lot. He took another swig of his beer, trying to figure out what kind of game Maymi was playing with Casper.

Was she actually interested in his brother?

There was no way in hell that his pesky neighbor could want

his brother Casper. He could tell from the way she was looking at him tonight at Sinful. So she must be trying to get to him through Casper and his brother was too arrogant to figure it out on his own.

Maymi was up to something and he would figure out what it was and put a stop to it before it went any further. He wasn't about to give either one of them any power to ruin his future. He wouldn't let her pretty eyes, sweet smile and delicious scent get under his skin any more than her curvy body had already done tonight.

Earlier tonight, he had been seconds away from kissing when she had been cleaning up his face. The touch of her soft hands against his skin was near intoxicating. A couple of times he almost had to tell her to stop because she was turning him on.

The light scent of vanilla that touched her skin filled his nose, making his cock take notice but he quickly shoved down his urges. Maymi wouldn't turn into Chloe for him...an unwanted distraction that would cloud his better judgment with her seductive young body and arresting looks.

Jensen remembered the days before he became a serious business owner. He wasn't ashamed to admit that he let his passions and desires take over for the years he worked as a male stripper. He was always safe and used a condom, but he loved the company of a beautiful woman when the desire had struck him.

Yet now, he wasn't a twenty-something year old boy anymore. He was no longer trying to get with all of the women he could because they were there for the taking. He had gotten a lot smarter and decided he needed to make a change in his life.

Back in the day, Jensen would have taken care of his Maymi problem in so many more pleasurable ways for the both of them. Since he was older and wiser, he learned to only take a woman to bed he cared about.

Only seeking a moment of hot, steamy, screaming orgasms was on the back burner. It took a lot of inner strength on his part, but he taught himself to resolve his temper and recklessness in other ways which had been a big help for him throughout the years.

Placing the empty beer bottle on the nightstand next to him, Jensen lay down on his bed and looked up through his skylight in his ceiling. He had always been fascinated by the stars even as a little boy when his father would show him the Big Dipper from their backyard.

Nothing relaxed him more than looking up and removing everything else from his thoughts especially after the day he had gone through. Dealing with Maymi's personality along with the two attackers would take down any other man even one as strong as him. Everybody had their breaking point.

Thank God he was off from work tomorrow and he could spend the day taking care of some personal matters. He hated the thought of leaving Casper in charge of his business, but he had to get some time off for himself before he worked himself into exhaustion and he had to be on his toes.

He wasn't sure what Maymi's next move might be but he would be ready for it, Jensen thought as he closed his eyes and tried relaxing to relieve some of the stiffness from his battered body

CHAPTER THIRTEEN

Four days later...

Walking down the health store food aisle, Maymi searched for the ingredients for her gluten free muffin and cupcakes. Sinful had been opened almost seven months tomorrow and she was getting requests now for these kinds of muffins which were understandable.

Researching how to correctly make them had taken her some time on the internet before she was able to find some basic recipes, then she added the Nana Monroe *'special touch'* to come up with two fantastic recipes. She had already been to three different stores until one of the cashiers told her about this place.

It was an hour drive from her house, but she was willing to make it for the benefit of her business. Luckily, if she could make these specialty treats as well as her non-gluten ones, more customers would come through the door.

Maymi pushed her cart further down the baking goods aisle and stopped in front of the gluten free items. She almost gasped out loud at some of the prices staring back at her in big black numbers.

Were these people out of their minds? Who in the hell would pay almost seven dollars for one bag of flour?

These prices were going to cut into her small budget fast, plus she still had about ten more items on her list and they were only for the muffins. The cupcakes needed four extra components that were on another sheet of paper in her back pocket.

The mere thought of digging into her already near empty pockets made Maymi's stomach drop to the bottom of her feet. Nevertheless, she was up to the challenge, so she grabbed the items off the shelf placing them inside of the cart.

She was more than confident that she would be able to think of a kick ass recipe for the healthy customers who had been coming into her store. She decided to start Sinful to draw all kinds of clientele and it was up to her to draw Jensen's health club clients into her bakery.

If she could make a low-fat, low calorie muffin, cupcake or cookie, they would flock to her bakery for an after work-out treat or maybe stop by for a snack during any day of the week. It was left up to her and no one else to make this happen.

Glancing down at the list in her hand, Maymi checked it to make sure that she wasn't forgetting anything in this aisle before moving on to the next item. She didn't want to drive way back out here for something simple.

"I know I must be seeing things because I know you aren't in a health food store. I didn't think you even knew any of these products existed."

Why did he have to be here today out of all days?

She hadn't laid eyes on him since the attack which was about three or four days ago. Jensen seemed to have the ability to ruin her good mood in the matter of seconds. God, how was it possible he was here with her?

Placing her list down in the cart, Maymi spun around trying not to stare at the muscles straining against the dark red t-shirt. Hell, she really hated how *hot* Jensen was. Usually guys who looked like him never got a second look from her, but for some stupid reason she couldn't stop noticing how good-looking he was all of the time.

Didn't this jerk know how to have an off day when it came to his looks?

"I hate to shock you, but yes I do know about this place. I'm working on some new baked goods for Sinful. I do know how to do more than one thing."

"Are you sure you're able to handle making healthy cookies, cakes and pies?" Jensen asked, his eyes watching her closely from underneath his baseball cap.

He had a way of making her uncomfortable from only a look. How was it possible for her to dislike him and then be drawn to his sorry ass a split second later? She was destined to be a guest of the Dr. Phil show.

"Yes, I can handle it if you must know," she snapped back. "God, you're getting on my last nerves with the way you're talking to me. I'm really kicking myself for helping you that night. My act of kindness sure hasn't made you think about being any nicer to me."

Maymi sighed and then spun around from Jensen. "Look, I have to go. Have a nice day. Mr. Lowe." She reached for her cart so she could leave, but a hand suddenly wrapped around her upper arm preventing her from moving anywhere.

"Don't go." Jensen sighed behind her. "I shouldn't have attacked you like that; it was wrong and thank you again for helping me. After the way I've been treating you I would have understood if you just drove away."

He let go of her arm and moved back from her personal space.

Don't accept his apology. Just keep walking and leave him standing there. Yet, she didn't do it because her father raised her not to be outright rude to anyone...not even Jensen.

Sighing, Maymi slowly pivoted and stared right back at him. *I can do this...Don't let him beat you*, she repeated to herself.

"You're welcome. I'm glad that I could help you. You seem like you're doing a lot better than the last time I saw you at Sinful."

"Yes, I am. I guess having you next door worked out for me that particular night," he said.

"Yeah, I guess it did. So now that means you are in my debt and will be until you do something life and death for me," she replied before turning around, then grabbed her cart walking away leaving Jensen staring after her with his mouth open.

~

Jensen tried not to smile, but the corners of his mouth turned up anyway. Maymi was so full of fight and determination. Her will to beat him was almost as attractive as her beautiful face, but not quite.

Today, she had pulled her hair back into a messy ponytail, tossed on a pair of black jeans that hugged her full ass way too good for his eyes not to stare as she sauntered away from him. Even her creamy, chocolate skin had a glow to it like she has just rolled out of bed after a good night of mind-fulfilling sex.

He couldn't help but wonder what guy put that look of satisfaction on her face he noticed when he was walking up on her before she noticed him there.

He would be lying to himself if he didn't admit that he noticed instantly how stunning Maymi was when she first came out of the kitchen door at Sinful. However, he shoved his instant attraction to her down because his visit had been based on business and getting a date with her hadn't been in his plans.

Foolishly he believed, after he laid out all of his concerns, Maymi would see reason and agree with him. Yet, she did the total opposite which only kicked up his competitive streak even more.

He wanted to get his way with her, but now he had something else to contend with because Maymi's unbending will had his cock hard. She turned him on more and more every time he was within hearing distance of her voice.

To make matter even worst for him, instead of being on his side, Casper decided to become her newest buddy. *So much for blood being thicker than water*, he thought.

Dealing with Maymi digging her tiny heels in was bad enough without his brother whispering encouraging words into her cute little ear.

Groaning, Jensen ran his hand down his face as something hit him. *Fuck!* Maymi had sidetracked him again.

Why was it every time he got around her she had the ability to make him lose track of time. He had to find a way to keep himself a step ahead of her 'sweet' personality with a hint of sin mixed in to distract him. Which would have to start with him not being too obvious about what he still wanted from her.

Hurrying around the corner, Jensen searched the aisles, hoping he would spot Maymi still inside of the store. He was about to give up until he saw her at the very end of the spice aisle. He kept walking until he was only standing a few inches behind her delectable body.

"Maymi, can I talk to you again?"

"Are you kidding me?"

He heard her mumble under her breath before she spun around and looked at him. "I thought we were finished. We both know where we stand with each other so why can't you just leave me alone?"

She started to turn away, but he caught her by the elbow spinning her back around. He wasn't fond of people turning their backs on him. She had already done it to him more than a few times, but it was going to stop today.

"Are you always so disagreeable?" Jensen asked, removing his hand when Maymi glared at him. "Or do I just bring that side of you out more?"

"No, I'm a pretty happy person but that is only to people who like me," she answered.

"I don't dislike you. I just think you need to take my advice."

"Oh, you don't have to say the words, it's written across your face every time you look at me."

Taking a step closer, Jensen blocked Maymi's body between the cart and his body. Her eyes blazed with sudden anger, but she didn't tell him to move away from her.

"How do you know I'm not thinking something else besides dislike when I'm looking at you?" he asked, lowering his voice. "You are a very good-looking woman. I would be fool not to notice."

Maymi blinked at him a second before she tossed her head back and her soft laughter filled the space around them.

"Are you kidding me?" She chuckled. "We both know you haven't paid attention to my looks once in all of the occasions our paths have crossed."

For a long moment, she looked back him while he stared back in waiting silence wondering what he was going to do with her. Maymi had a mouth on her and someone should have taught her a long time ago how to think more and talk less.

She needed to be tamed...she was a little *too wild* with her words for him.

"What's wrong? Have I shocked you speechless with my com—"

Jensen kissed Maymi, stealing the rest of the words from her mouth. He captured her moist lips with his, demanding a response. He was tired of her pretending she knew what his next move was going to be, it was time to show Maymi who was in the driver's seat and it sure wasn't *her*.

His tongue licked at the corner of her mouth before she acknowledged his request and opened her lips giving him entrance to her hidden treasure. Slowly, he traced his tongue along the recesses of her mouth as his cock hardened against the zipper of his suddenly too tight jeans. He gave her a few more nibbling kisses then raised his mouth before things got out of hand.

Usually, he wasn't fond of PDA, but Maymi brought out sides of him he never knew existed until he stared in her chocolate eyes. He noticed the confusion mingled with unleashed desire simmering there.

"Wh...Wh...What do you think you are doing?" she demanded her lips swollen from his kisses.

"Showing you that you can never figure out what is going on inside of my head, so don't even try. I will prove you wrong every time, Brown Eyes." He brushed another kiss across her surprised mouth before spinning around and walking away first this time, leaving as flabbergasted Maymi watching him leave.

Chapter Fourteen

"Tatum, it took everything in my power not to slap his smug face," Maymi complained as she pulled another tray of low fat cookies out of the oven and closed the door with her elbow. "I swear that man acts like every woman with a pulse should fall at his feet."

"I think you're complaining way too much," Tatum said from behind her as she transferred the oatmeal raisin cookies to a cooling rack.

"I mean, are you really upset a guy hotter than most Hollywood actors kissed you in the middle of a store? Come on, it's me you're talking to, not Jazmaine. I saw how you were checking Jensen out at the restaurant. I can understand why because he's super hot!"

Walking over to the table, Maymi worked on mixing up the last batch of cookie batter. She used a small ice cream scoop and placed the balls of dough on a sheet tray before taking it over to the oven. Opening it, she slid them inside, closed the door and set the timer.

She opened her mouth and then snapped it closed. She wanted to lie, but she couldn't.

Jensen's shocking kiss was so good it almost had her moaning and begging him not to stop. Why was it the guy who a woman wanted to hate? Somehow, he was the one who constantly made her panties wet.

"Alright, I was checking out Jensen," Maymi admitted as she looked back over at Tatum. "However, it doesn't give him the right to think he can kiss me to prove a point or stroke his already over swollen ego."

Leaning across the work counter, Tatum picked up a no bake cookie and waved it at her. "Did his kiss take your breath away? Do you even know what that is? I don't ever recall you talking about a man since Hudson."

She wasn't going to talk about Hudson or compare him to Jensen. Hudson had been the most loving, caring and supportive man she ever had in her life. Maymi blinked away sudden tears. She couldn't let herself get dragged back into the memories.

"Yes, his kiss stole my breath away. I've had time to date and even to get kissed but none of their kisses compared to his. It was shocking and I hate to admit a small part of me wanted it to continue. Yet, I think... No, I know he kissed me for another reason besides wanting to prove a point."

"Honey, don't care about why Jensen's gorgeous mouth touched yours. All I would do is pray every night for it to happen again."

Maymi rolled her eyes wondering what she was going to do with Tatum. Her best friend always went for what was in her face instead of going for the bigger picture.

"What am I doing to do with you?" she asked.

"Listen to my wonderful advice," Tatum suggested then took a bite of the cookie in her hand. "Mmmm. This is so good. Can I have another one for the road? You make these to tempt my willpower, don't you?"

"Yes, I do, along with everyone else who has a sweet tooth," Maymi answered.

Walking across the kitchen, she grabbed a small hot pink cookie box off the shelf and then added a few extra cookies inside for Tatum. "Here you go. Don't eat them all in one day. Save some for tomorrow," she teased, handing her friend the box.

Tatum took the box from her. "Girl, these are adorable," she said, running her hand over the lettering on the top. "I love the look of them, very eye-catching."

"Thank you. I'm almost out of them because business has been so red hot," Maymi gushed. "Honestly, since the last time we had dinner together, Sinful has improved even more."

"Sweetheart, you deserve all of this success. I told you not to listen to your father. He doesn't have a clue what a talented pastry chef you are. Didn't you come in second place on *Incredible Desserts* and then took first place on *Monster Cookies*? You're very gifted and the best friend I could ask for."

"We have been through a lot together, haven't we?" Walking

up to Tatum, she gave her a hug then stepped back. "Thank you for always being my sounding board. I can tell you anything."

"Honey, you know I have been keeping your dirty secrets for years, so I'm not about to stop this late in our lives."

"You better not." Maymi laughed, linking her arms through Tatum's. "Let me walk you out before I need to start working on these low-fat cupcakes."

Maymi walked through the door, hoping this new recipe worked for her. She wanted them to be a hot seller like her grandmother's other desserts, but she was a concerned the taste might not be up to par with the rich old school ones.

"Make some extra ones so Jazmaine and I can be your tasters. You know your girls will tell you the truth. Just like I did about you liking the spontaneous kiss Jensen planted on you. All I have to say is, if it happens again, kiss his handsome butt back," Tatum encouraged before turning around and going out of the door.

She loved Tatum even with her over-giving advice side, but she wasn't going to listen to one word that came from her mouth about Jensen. The kiss he gave her was good...no exceptional...one of the best she had in a very *long* time, but she couldn't let him seduce her emotions again especially not out in a public or alone.

They just shared a momentary lapse in judgment which neither one of them probably wanted to experience again. Yeah, Jensen better watch his step because the next time he tried something like his kiss again, he might get a surprise from her he wasn't expecting.

Maymi took a minute to flip the *'Gone to lunch'* sign back over to *'Yes, we're Open.'* She needed to spend more time actually sitting down to eat lunch instead of sneaking a bite here and there in the back while she was baking. She moved away from the door and was halfway across the room when the bell chimed above the door, making her turn back around.

"Great, you're open," a tall, gray haired man said. He wore an expensive dark blue suit, and hurried over to the cupcake display case. "How many cupcakes are in there?"

"I have a little over two dozen," Maymi answered, going behind the counter.

"I'll take all of them along with all of your chocolate chip cookies. "I need them for a retirement party at my office. My assistant was praising your goodies and she's the pickiest sweets eater in the world. So I know if she loves the things here they must be first-rate."

"Thank you. I make them myself," Maymi said as she boxed up everything and rang it up for the man. She gave him the price then took the platinum credit card he handed her.

"I hope you enjoy everything and please come again." She gave the gentleman his four boxes along with his receipt and card back.

"Oh, I don't have a doubt I won't and you have a nice day," he told her then left as quickly as he came in.

For the next several hours, Maymi worked on the steady flow of customers that came through the doors of Sinful with a bounce to her step. The rush of customers is what she wished for during her grand opening and finally weeks later, it was here. Her day couldn't possibly get any better if she wrote the script of it herself.

Taking a towel from the waistband of her apron, she began wiping the few crumbs off the counter that came from handing out free cookies to the kids. She bent down and pulled out all of the empty trays placing them behind her on the counter just as the bell above the door chimed again.

"Give me a minute and I'll be right with you," Maymi called out as she finished stacking up the last of the trays.

"Should I feel insulted that my kiss was so lackluster that it didn't have you next door warning me to stay away from you or else?" a familiar voice questioned behind her. "Maybe I should give it another try to get the reaction I wanted."

Maymi felt her pulse jump as Tatum's words rushed back to haunt her, but she shoved them down just as fast.

"I believe I told you before if you showed up here again uninvited, I would toss you out without thinking twice about it," she countered, twirling to find Jensen standing on the other side of her dessert counter.

"I've been in here since then and you were very nice to me," Jensen reminded her in his rich, deep voice that she was starting to hear in her dreams. "So your threats don't scare me anymore. Besides, I believe I could take you."

"Don't let my size fool you. I'm tougher than I look." Coming around the edge of the counter, Maymi stopped in front of Jensen, trying not to get lost in his masculinity, but it was extremely hard since it seemed to surround everything about him.

"I know you didn't come over here to exchange small talk with me so what can I do for you?" she asked, hoping Jensen couldn't see how excited she was to see him.

Damn Tatum and Jazmaine for giving her all of that stupid advice now she couldn't keep it out of her head with Jensen standing right within touching distance of her fingers.

Chapter Fifteen

Jensen's eyes sparkled at her as he crossed his arms over his wide, muscular chest. "You're always brewing for a fight, aren't you? Did you ever think I might just have come over here to see your pretty face?" he asked, shocking her, but Maymi quickly recovered.

"I'm betting Fitness 24 has several pretty women for you to find appealing so why don't you tell me the truth?"

Numerous ideas raced through her head as to why Jensen was standing in front of her. One thing was for sure: this guy was full of surprises and she hated surprises, especially when they didn't benefit her but him.

"You're right. My gym does have a lot of gorgeous women over there, but I think you are a lot more interesting than they are. I never know what's going to come out of your mouth and a part of me likes that about you."

Something clicked in Maymi's head and she was beginning to see where Jensen was going with this. Did he think she was so gullible that she would fall for his new tactic? She was a little disappointed he thought so little of her to do this.

"You have a lot of nerve, don't you," she said. "I mean your threats didn't work on me because I was too strong. You saw another chance to manipulate me at the health food store with an unwanted kiss that wasn't anything to write home about."

God, she hoped he believed that huge lie! She noticed how Jensen uncrossed his arms and took a small step in her direction. Maybe he did because he looked pissed as hell with her.

"I didn't hear you complaining at the store about my kissing abilities or the lack of them," he tossed back. "Brown eyes, I saw your face and you liked it. You wanted me to continue."

"How could I? You kissed me so quickly I couldn't shove you away and tell you how bad it was. It would have torn down your fragile ego. Guys like you work out because you can't do anything else with your life."

Jensen's rich hazel's eyes grew a shade darker as soon as the words left her mouth and Maymi wondered if she should have kept her mouth shut and just walked away.

"I believe you are denying our kiss way too much, Ms. Monroe. I think you got into it more than you want to admit to me and more importantly yourself," Jensen taunted, softly.

His arrogance was going to be his downfall with me, Maymi thought.

No matter what Jensen did, she wasn't ever going to give him the inch he was trying to get out of her. "You'll be waiting forever if you think I'm going to admit I like you."

"I don't need you to admit anything to me. You might be denying it now, but you kissed me back. Sure, we might be arguing but we both know our arguing is—"

The bell chimed above the door and Maymi quickly slipped around Jensen as the tension began to get a little too thick between them. She would be extra nice to whoever the person was who just showed up and stopped her from kissing Jensen first this time.

"Good morning, can I help—?" Her eyes widened at the sight of Casper standing there holding two boxes.

"Casper, what are you doing here? I wasn't expecting to see you today."

What in the hell was going on this morning? She couldn't figure out why Jensen was even here because seeing him was a total surprise.

His eyes darted over to Jensen then back over to her. "Am I interrupting something?" Casper asked, staring at her.

She didn't like the confused look on his face. It looked like he was reading more into the situation than there really was. She wasn't doing anything with Jensen. They had only been talking and nothing else.

"Actually your timing is perfect since your brother and I were about to get into another useless argument over nothing." Maymi glanced over her shoulder making eye contact with Jensen. "Was there anything else you wanted from me?"

Jensen cocked one eyebrow at her. "No, I guess there wasn't since you aren't capable of having an adult conversation with me. I'll leave so you can talk to my brother instead of me since the two of you seem to have grown *so* close."

He brushed past her and then paused in front of Casper. She could tell from his body language Jensen wasn't pleased his conversation with her had gotten taken over by his brother's surprise appearance.

"Don't waste too much time over here. We need to have a staff meeting in twenty minutes and I want you to be there," Jensen said then literally stormed away, went out the door without looking back at either one of them.

"I swear he's constantly in a bad mood," Maymi complained. "I think he hates seeing me every day."

"I think the problem is bigger than you. Jensen is a great guy, but he takes on too much sometimes. He needs to cut loose more, but I didn't come here to discuss him. I've a present for you."

Excitement raced through Maymi's veins as she took the boxes from Casper. She couldn't image what was on the inside. She hadn't known him long enough to be getting gifts from him.

"What's in here? Should I be getting presents from you?" she asked, walking over to a small table.

"Why don't you open them up and find out?" Casper suggested.

Not wasting another minute, she opened the large box gasping at the bakery boxes on the inside with Sinful designed across the top in beautiful black lettering. She was speechless. Maymi swallowed a few times trying to regain her composure.

"Do you like them?" Casper asked, leaning over her shoulder. "I still felt bad for ruining the other ones, so I had these made to take care of the ones I couldn't fix."

"My God...these are beautiful but they're too expensive. I mean the lettering alone would put me back two months. I can't accept them. It wouldn't be right." Maymi tried reclosing the lid, but Casper's hand shot out and stopped her.

"I won't take them back. Besides, my buddy who did them owed me a favor and I got them at a discount. There's also another reason I got these made for you," he admitted, softly.

Taken back by the sudden change in Casper's usually carefree voice, Maymi turned around and was caught off guard by the serious look in his eyes.

"If you hadn't helped my brother that night something could have happened to him. I know Jensen has been a pain in your ass about your bakery. You could have ignored his situation and walked away and not one person would have known about it.

"He can be a hard man to like, even love, when he's trying to get his point across, but I love my brother. I don't tell him that enough and I probably won't ever confess it unless I'm really pushed. However, I still have him here trying to dictate my every move and I've you to thank for that. Thank you."

She opened her mouth to say something but no words came out. How was she supposed to tell him something after that little confession? Who knew Casper could be so deep?

"Hey, I made you speechless and that usually only happens after a woman sees me naked," he joked.

Snap. Maymi was suddenly jerked out of her world of silence. Only Casper could bring up sex inside of a bakery.

"Alright, I think you need to leave," she said, giving him a small shove in the shoulder. "You are preventing me from finishing up the last of my orders. I can't have your crazy humor side-tracking me."

"Oh, you'll be thinking about me all day," Casper teased, wiggling his eyebrows. "Unless, it's my brooding brother who has captured your attention; I noticed how the two of you were awful close before I came through the door. It was so hot I almost walked away."

"If there's anything hot in Sinful, it's the oven and nothing else," Maymi denied as she opened the door and shoved Casper outside to the sidewalk.

"Come on, sweetness. I know my brother can be a complete jerk; but he was blessed in the looks department. Of course, not as much as me but certain woman find that dark, tortured soul look of his sexy."

Maymi honestly didn't know what to say. Casper was either out of his mind or loved pushing her to the edge when it came to Jensen. Either way, she wasn't going to take the bait because he was seeing something that wasn't there.

"Okay, time for you to leave for real now," she told him. Maymi tried to closing the front door but a huge size thirteen shoe wedged its shelf inside the door.

"Alright, I apologize for teasing you about my brother. I can't get the best baker in Wyoming mad at me. Can you forgive me?" Big, blue eyes stared at her followed by a crooked, boyish grin.

"God, you are incorrigible." Maymi laughed, rolling her eyes. "How can I stay mad at you? I forgive you."

"I knew you would," Casper bragged then removed his foot and turned, going down the sidewalk towards his job.

Maymi watched her new buddy walk away until his back rounded the corner. Thankfully, Casper hadn't seen through her lie when she told him she wasn't attracted to his brother.

She'd wanted him since the first day she laid eyes on him. She just had to make sure she kept a tight rein on her desire. She couldn't have it go anywhere not what was at stake. Maymi knew exactly how to deal with Jensen and the sooner she dealt with him the better. The only way to make sure he understood was to tell Jensen to his face.

Chapter Sixteen

Slamming his office door behind him, Jensen's pulse pounded away inside of his ears as he recalled how Maymi's face had lit up once she saw Casper saunter through the door. He wasn't used to this feeling eating at him. Not once in his life had he and Casper been drawn to the same woman.

He could still taste her mouth on his and he was seconds away from another sample, but Casper had to pick that moment to barge in on them.

Hell, what was going on with him?

How could one kiss have him turned inside out like this? He had kissed plenty of women before, but something about the short time he had tasted Maymi was different. He hadn't wanted to stop; if they hadn't been out in public he would have continued kissing that pretty mouth of hers for hours.

What was it about her that had him twisted up in such knots? One minute all he could think about was making her disappear from his life entirely. However, after the kiss he planted on her he couldn't help wondering how it would be to have her in his bed.

Jensen stopped cold in his tracks. No! The thought entered his head before he could stop it, just like the kiss, but he wasn't going to act on it. He had control over his weak willpower. He spent years getting his body in top shape. Yet, he wasn't able to control his *craving* for her.

Why she sparked this side of him was something he couldn't understand. Truthfully, he actually liked how the flame came into her brown eyes when they fought. The sound of her raised voice made his cock hard. So much that he couldn't think of anything else but taking her to the nearest bed and having his way with her.

His cock grew ever harder and thicker thinking about Maymi's tight, spunky body as he made love to her for hours until she forgot all about his brother. Being jealous of another man wasn't in his DNA.

Yet, when he saw how happy Casper made Maymi, the woman who literally hated the sound of his voice, something changed inside of him. For some stupid reason, he couldn't figure out why he wanted Maymi to look at him the same way. The reaction had to be a sibling rivalry thing. He and Casper were always competitive. Why should this be any different?

Fuck, what kind of body snatchers had taken over his body in the middle of the night? He hated Maymi…Well, hate was *too* strong of a word, but he was worried about her abilities not to steal his clients away over to her world of delectable pleasures.

He hated he wanted her physically, but he couldn't control the erection that appeared anytime her tempting body was hovering near his. Taking her wasn't part of anything he wanted and his mind knew it, but his dick had other plans that his head couldn't override.

A sudden knock on his office door jarred Jensen from another, unwanted ridiculous thought about Maymi. He walked over to the door wondering who was bothering him this early. He thought he had got everything answered in the staff meeting twenty minutes ago.

"Yeah, what can I do for you," he asked, opening the door.

His eyes widened from shock when they landed on Maymi standing there. *Why did she have to show up now?* Smelling like vanilla, cinnamon, sugar and everything sexy to push his sexual drive up another dangerous notch without her even knowing what she was doing.

"Is there something I can do for you?" Jensen asked, placing his hand against the doorframe. He had to do something with his hand or he might break down and give in to his urge to take over her senses with another kiss.

"Yes, we need to talk and I'm not leaving until we get everything out in the open," Maymi said. She slipped underneath his arm and strolled into his personal space like she owned it.

Jensen moved away from the door and slowly closed it and then locked it for good measure. He couldn't let anyone walk in on them. Casper had already done it once today and a repeat performance wasn't about to happen.

He and Maymi needed to hash everything out because this back and forth between them was getting old very fast. She might not realize it but he was a grown man. Jensen had ever been fond of playing games with women. So he wasn't about to start it now with the package of dynamite standing in front of him waiting to explode.

Slowly, Jensen made his way to Maymi, crossing the distance between them. He liked how he was taller than her five feet two inches. His height gave him some advantage that her sharp tongue couldn't take away from him. She might be able to fight back with her words, but this one battle she would never win over him.

"Okay, princess. Why did you grace me with your presence again so soon?" he asked, watching how her big chocolate eyes shot up to his. Jensen crossed his arms over his chest and waited for an answer.

"I came to tell you to stop trying all of your head games on me, because they aren't going to work. I'm a lot tougher than I look and you aren't man enough to handle me, big boy."

Uncrossing his arms, he leaned down until he was face to face with Maymi. He wasn't a man to back down from such a blatant invitation tossed in his face. He had to give her credit for having enough nerve to do it right in his office without batting an eye.

"Princess, I'm all man and if you *ever* need proof I'll be more than pleased to give it to you," he promised, softly.

"Take your ego down a notch, Jensen," she said, patting him in the middle of his chest.

The soft touch of her hand made his dick throb to the point of being painful. Grabbing her wrist, he jerked Maymi against his chest. The feel of her full breasts against his chest almost made him growl with pleasure, but he caught the sound seconds before it betrayed him. He made a mental note to stay in control when it came to this spitfire.

CHAPTER SEVENTEEN

"Let go of me," Maymi snapped, tugging at her wrist. "I came over here to have a conversation, not get into another fight."

"I never said I wanted to fight with you. I thought we were talking about our kiss. You were going to tell me how much you loved it."

She snickered. "How could I have loved something that was so dull? I swear after it was over I had forgotten it ever happened. I've had better kisses from—

Before Maymi had a chance to insult him again, Jensen spun her around and pressed her back against the closet wall capturing her mouth with his. He realized this seemed to be the only way to stop that tongue of her from mouthing off to him. Running his tongue along the corner of her mouth, he took advantage of her surprise gasp by slipping his tongue inside.

Good God, she tasted so good.

He let go of her wrist and spread her thighs with his knees stepping between them. He *never* had a sweet tooth before but the honeyed taste of Maymi's mouth was giving him a bad one!

"You taste like honey," he breathed against her swollen lips. He couldn't help but take some pride in her body's reaction to his kisses.

"It's from my tea," Maymi whispered, easing back from him and staring into his eyes.

Jensen's cock jerked at the smoky desire he saw there. He shouldn't be enjoying this tugging attraction his body felt towards her, but hell he did. So what was he going to do about it?

"Don't move," he said, placing his hands on either side of her hips, blocking her against the wall. He liked the feel of her curves. They were a lot different than Chloe's rail thin figure.

"What are we going? What are you trying to prove?" Maymi

asked. "None of this is making any sense."

"I'm only trying to show you I can handle anything you toss in my direction. Don't you have anything to say? No sharp comeback... This isn't like you. Ms. Maymi Monroe is never speechless in my company." Jensen moved back from her so he wouldn't give in to the urge to start kissing her luscious mouth again.

He wondered what she was thinking. The air around them was sizzling with white hot temptation, but Maymi was silent as a church mouse. He didn't know if he should be thrilled he finally got her to stop talking or be pissed as hell his kiss made her completely mute.

❧❦

How could she let Jensen kiss her again?

The second time was even better than the first, but it didn't matter. Both had caught her completely off guard shattering her self-control. Pressing her fingers against her swollen lips, Maymi gazed at Jensen in a daze of confusion. She couldn't find the words to discuss how his mouth made her feel.

So yes... She guessed the 'cat' did have her tongue and now she was trying to figure out how to get it back from his master—the smug devil standing in front of her with a huge hard-on pressed against the front of his tight jeans.

None of this...Shit!

She couldn't even form a complete thought because of him. Panic set in...she had to get out of here. She was twenty-eight years too old to be experiencing sexual frustration from a guy she thought about slapping most of the time.

Every time they were together Jensen took over their meeting like he owned it and her. She came over here to best him and the devil ended up getting the better of her. The realization of that didn't please her at all. She had to get away from him unless she wanted to give up what tiny bit of willpower she had left in order to regroup. That was the only reason she was leaving... the only one.

Yeah, keep telling yourself that, girl.

"Mmmm...I need to go. Olivia is probably wondering what happened to me. I only came over here to give the cakes time to cool."

Maymi eased away from the wall and around Jensen. She stumbled and would have fallen if Jensen's large hands hadn't reached out and caught her in time.

"Watch yourself. I can't have anything happening to you now because if you're hurt I won't have anyone to argue with at least twice a week," he teased.

She shook off Jensen's touch and then took a step away from him. He was purposely trying to sneak under her defenses and trick her with his hot kisses, roaming hands and deep hypnotic voice but she would continue to fight him.

"Mr. Lowe, you would love for something to happen to me because Sinful's space would be yours for the taking."

Sliding his hand behind her neck, Jensen eased her body closer to his. Her breath caught in the back of her throat as Jensen's gorgeous eyes never left hers for an instant.

"Have you realized since you walked through my office door, I haven't brought up either one of our businesses? I've better things I would rather be doing with you and discussing them isn't even in the same realm."

She ran her tongue over her suddenly dry lips as Jensen's thumb stroked her jaw igniting her awareness of his sexuality even more. Instantly, his bedroom brown eyes grew a shade darker as he cupped her chin inside his warm palm.

Her hand moved of its own volition, touching Jensen's cheek down to his strong jaw line. "This is so crazy," she whispered. "I can't explain it, but I'm drawn to you. As much as we fight, our arguments haven't made it any less intense."

Jensen's gaze was riveted on her face, and then moved over her body slowly before his eyes recaptured hers. She tried to push down the racing current pounding through her body, but couldn't. He was stroking a gently growing flame and knew it.

"Have dinner with me tonight."

Maymi knew her desire for Jensen had nothing to do with reason. It was too easy to get lost in the way he was looking at her; however, some of the things he had spoken to her were still in the back of her mind which made it hard for her to just forgive and forget so easily.

Touching Jensen's wrist, she removed it away from her face and stepped round his tempting, rippling body again. The power radiating from him was very intoxicating to her weakening senses. Accepting a dinner invitation from him would only muddy her thoughts concerning them even more. She wasn't ready to stare into his amazing eyes across a candlelight dinner.

"I can't go out on a date with you," she answered. "That isn't a part of the game we play with each other."

He frowned at her. "I wasn't aware we were playing any sort of games with each other. I asked you out on a date and I want to know the truth why you won't accept it. Are you frightened you wouldn't be able to handle something that wasn't here or Sinful? I promise to be gentle and walk you through it unless there's another reason for your backtracking."

"Like what?" Maymi asked, staring at Jensen with a clueless expression.

Chapter Eighteen

"Casper," Jensen replied wondering if Maymi would deny it. He was more than enough man to push his brother or any other man out of her mind today or any other day of the week.

"No, your brother wasn't even on my mind," she said. "Which means he can't be the reason I'm turning you down."

"Are you still trying to make me believe my kisses do nothing for you, baby?" he asked, lowering his voice.

He watched how Maymi's eyes darted over to the door like she was thinking about making a run for it which wasn't something he was used to seeing from her. She usually stood toe to toe with him.

"After the way I responded to your kiss again wouldn't it be stupid of me to lie to you a second time?" she answered.

"Fine, if neither one of those are the reasons, tell me what is. I can't read your mind. I need something to work with here and only you can give it to me."

"You hate me," Maymi blurted out. "We both know it's true. Unlike you, I can't allow a few exceptional kisses blind me to the truth right in front of me. We know how to push each other's buttons because the attraction we experienced the first time our eyes connected at Sinful."

"Maymi, I don't hate you," he instantly disagreed.

Jensen knew he hadn't been the nicest guy to her, but he didn't hate her. He wouldn't admit it to her, but her toughness was very impressive. No matter what he had thrown at her she had given it right back to him. She was proving to him that she was more than a pretty face.

Maymi's quick wit kept him on his toes and looking forward to what would come out of her pretty mouth next.

Her comments had them in a war of words which Jensen found to be a complete turn-on from his end of things, but it seemed like Maymi's interruption of the events was totally different than his. She thought he hated her, but hate was too strong of a word to use in trying to figure out their relationship.

Sometimes when she wouldn't listen he felt like shaking some sense into her or kissing her senseless, but he didn't hate her at all. She was probably the most intoxicating distraction that he had met in a very long time.

"Maymi, you have misunderstood me," Jensen said. "We may fight, but I don't hate you."

"I know you aren't fond of me, and if you had three wishes, you would use one of those to send me and Sinful far away from you way across town. Don't deny it," she said.

Without warning, Jensen's hand wrapped around Maymi's waist gently tugging her to him until they were only inches apart. He noticed a strange, faintly eager look flash in her eyes as she watched him and waited.

"You're right. I would use one of the wishes but not like you're thinking. I would wish for you to stop being so inflexible with me and agree to a date. I mean, if you can handle my brother's nonsense, going out with me should be a piece of cake. Just think how it could be if we found out we might actually become friends."

Maymi shook her head. "The problem isn't Casper, it's you. The two of you are like on totally different ends of the scale when it comes to how you treat me. When your brother first met me and told me his last name, I thought I had misheard."

Enough was enough!

He was done wasting his time with Maymi talking about his charming little brother. He wasn't blessed with that characteristic and he was done wishing that he had been. He had his own traits that were equally or more attractive to draw Maymi over to his side.

"I know my brother isn't me and I'm proud of that fact. Casper is still a boy while I'm a full grown man. You look like a woman who likes having a man around her, so what is your answer. Are you ready to test our ability to have a date?"

Maymi tilted her head to the side and Jensen could read the interest in her eyes. He saw that she wanted to take him up on it, but wasn't sure. He had to make her agree or he wasn't using this golden opportunity to the fullest.

"How about I promise not to talk about either one of our businesses on the entire date? We just can try to have a good time with each other. I'm game if you are unless you're scared that you might actually have a good time with your enemy. What's your answer, princess?" he asked.

Jensen smiled when Maymi's chin went up and her eyes glared at him. *Finally*...the determined, feisty look he had actually liked getting from her. The meek Maymi wasn't his favorite. She had too much fire inside of her to be backing off from one date with him. He wasn't afraid to pursue their intense reaction to each other.

"I'm still not sure if we could handle being around each other on an actual date," she admitted. "You know how we are with each other. Sparks just seem to fly when we least expect it."

Leaning closer, he got right in her face. "I can't deny I like our fireworks, so why not take it out on the road. I'm more than up for it, but if you're nervous I'll understand and let it go."

Maymi laughed. A soft, sexy sound that made him hornier than he already was. "Fine, I'll go out on a date with you."

"How about tonight?" Jensen asked. He wasn't going to give her any time to think about it more and have another chance to change her mind.

"I can't tonight," she said, placing her hand in the center of his chest pushing him back. "I already have plans after work. How about Friday? I'm closing the bakery early, probably around noon."

He wanted to push for tonight since everything was going so well between them, but he wouldn't. This date was a test to see if he could get a second date with her. Maymi possessed a lot more substance than any other woman who had been in his life.

Jensen knew the only way to get her to let her 'keep Jensen away' barriers down was to do it in a neutral environment like a date or walk through the park. He was hungry to discover more about what made her tick.

She had already given him hints about what treasures lay deep within her. It fascinated him even more when he watched how open she was around other people but him.

"Friday is good for me. I can wait until I get to see you in something besides jeans and a Sinful t-shirt," he admitted, staring into Maymi's eyes almost getting lost in the beauty of them.

"I could tell you the same thing," she flirted back. The tension in the room started getting thicker and hotter the more they continued staring at each other. "I'm wondering how your body is going to look all dressed up for our date."

Taking a step closer and then another one until he could feel Maymi's chest touching his, he stared at her without breaking eye contact. "If you weren't so stubborn and decided to make me wait until Friday you would get to see how good I look in a suit."

"I think I'll be able to handle the wait. Patience is a virtue, so it will give me something to look forward to this weekend," she said, running her finger down the center of his chest.

Grabbing her by the hips, he yanked Maymi completely against him. "Keep tempting me and I won't be able to keep from doing what I want to do."

There was an eagerness in her eyes he hadn't noticed before when she looked at him, but he wouldn't mind seeing again. Yet, he had to get her out of his office before things went too far, more than he allowed in the work place.

"You better go before I forget I'm a gentleman and kiss the hell out of that beautiful mouth of yours," Jensen admitted. He was losing control fast and Maymi was the only reason for his lack of concentration.

"Alright, I do need to get out of here. I need to call Tatum to recheck out plans for tonight," she said, touching the side of his cheek.

"Who is Tatum?" How many men did she have falling around her? First, his brother and now some guy named Tatum. Was he ever going to get a chance to get her alone and away from everyone else?

"Tatum is one of my best friends. We try to get together at least twice a month. So I'm not canceling my plans with her."

Tatum was a female...he couldn't believe it, but he wasn't about to let Maymi know he thought she was a he. He didn't want to admit he might have been jealous of someone else. It was bad enough he had gotten the green eyed monster with Casper.

"I guess I can let you go out with Tatum, but you have to do one thing for me before you leave."

Her left eyebrow raised a fraction as she continued watching him. "I'm afraid to ask what you might want, Mr. Lowe," she teased.

"It's nothing that will hurt," Jensen whispered, lowering his head until their lips were a breath apart. "All I want is this."

Reclaiming her mouth, he slid his hand through her hair holding, Maymi still while he got lost in the sweetness of her mouth. God! He never got this disoriented in kissing any other woman like he did with her. He could kiss Maymi for hours and never get tired.

Jensen wanted to continue but the moan of ecstasy that slipped for Maymi's lips brought him back. Shit! He hadn't made out with a female like this since college and Sarah Willis was his steady girlfriend until she dumped him for her professor.

"Why are you making it so hard on me to let you leave?" he whispered against her cheek.

"I want to give you something to keep you on your toes until our date," Maymi said before pushing him away from her. "Now I really need to go now. I've been gone way too long. I know I've baked goodies I need to make. I can drop my address off after work." She started to walk away from him, but he grabbed her by the arm.

"No, wait. Let me give you my phone number and you can text me your information." Moving away from Maymi, Jensen grabbed a small piece of paper off his desk and wrote down his number. "Here you go." He spun back around and handed her the sheet of paper.

"Thank you," Maymi said. She took the paper from his hand and slipped it into the front pocket of her jeans. "I hope you're ready to blow me away on Friday. I haven't been impressed in a long time."

"You didn't go out with me, so anything I do Friday will be better than everything any other man has done for you," Jensen replied with confidence.

"Let me be the judge of that," Maymi tossed back. Turning away from him, she walked over to his office door and went out without looking back.

Leaning against his desk, Jensen looked at the open door, oblivious to the smile of his face. Maymi intrigued him since he laid eyes on her. He was finally ready to admit that he might see a tiny bit of himself in her.

It could be one of the reasons they went at it so well with each other. Each one knew actually what button to push on the other one, but he wouldn't be sure until their date on Friday. Today was only

Wednesday. Could he make it through another day until he finally got Maymi alone?

Well, he agreed to wait and that is what he would do as much as he didn't want to do it. Moving away from his desk, Jensen walked around and took a seat behind it. He couldn't let his entire day consist of thinking about his upcoming date with her. Friday would be here soon enough.

Besides, the pile of please call slips on his desk weren't going to answer themselves. However, he had to make one call before the rest. He knew he hadn't heard from Jack, so he would have to contact him. His business goals still had to keep moving forward until he finally got all of his ducks in a row, and gaining the Health Pro's building was now at the top of his list.

Picking up the telephone at his left, Jensen started calling Jack's phone number when suddenly a knock on his office door stopped him. Turning his head, he was surprised to see Jack standing there in the doorway.

"Do you have a minute?" he asked. "I need to talk to you."

Wondering what was going on, Jensen placed the phone back down and he waved Jack into his office. He hoped he wasn't going to ask for more money because Health Pro wasn't worth more than he offered him. If he did then this deal would be over.

"Sure, I was just about to call you. Come on in and shut the door," Jensen said secretly hoping this guy was ready to sign on the dotted line.

"I've a few things I want to go over first," Jack said, closing the door.

"Have a seat and I'll see what I can do for you."

Whatever the reason Jack showed up here at Fitness 24, he wasn't about to let on how much he wanted his failing business. He would let him talk and see what his terms were before he completely shut anything down.

❧❧

As she drove home from Sinful after spending the past ten hours working on getting out two surprise cupcakes orders, Maymi finally allowed her mind to wander back to her kissing session with Jensen. She wondered if the heat from her ovens had finally caused her to lose her mind.

Something had to be wrong up there in that brain of hers to make her agree to a date with *him*. She should have turned Jensen down flat, but once she gazed into those brown eyes of his she got lost and then once he kissed her again she was a goner and they both knew it.

Damn...why hadn't she listened to her first instinct and kept from going over to Fitness 24 in the first place? Why was she even bothering thinking about this when she already knew the answer? She wanted to have the last word.

The way Jensen had demanded for Casper not to waste a lot of time with her hadn't sat right, so after he left instead of letting it go and moving on with her day she had to take her butt over there thinking she would get the upper hand.

However, Jensen kissed that idea out of her head and seduced her into agreeing to a date with him. Thank God, she was quick enough to at least think of a lie and get it pushed back into Friday. She didn't have plans with Tatum because her girlfriend was out of town of business. She might be able to think of an excuse not to go by then.

Are you scared of what you might do? The question entered her head and left just as fast.

No! Maymi wasn't afraid of going out on one little date with Jensen Lowe. She would be able to handle this like anything else he tried tossing her way. She was unbreakable, but hell, she still needed one of her girlfriends to vent with about this new situation.

Why wasn't Jazmaine answering her stupid phone? She had already called her twice and got her voice mail. She had even left two text messages for her. She needed her other best friend right now to unload on and she wasn't anywhere around. What was going on with Jazmaine?

Chapter Nineteen

Jazmaine read Maymi's text message while she waited for Mr. Akito Mashiro's assistant to show up to finalize the last of the paperwork to hire him. Mr. Kent wanted him as the graphic novel writer/artist for their upcoming series, but this was getting on her nerves.

For the past five months they had been going back and forth trying to please Mr. Mashiro's every demand, but if she had one more complaint from him. She would take herself off this deal and someone else at the office could handle it from this point on.

Working all of these long hours just to stroke this guy's ego was getting way out of hand for her liking. She hadn't been able to do anything else with her free time but take care of this man's every whim. Especially when it came to tiny details in the multi-million dollar contracts Mr. Kent needed signed, yet she wouldn't actually quit because her boss was counting on her to get everything done.

Getting Mr. Mashiro to even agree to think about doing a four book graphic novel deal with them was huge. So she understood why her boss was bending over backwards to give him everything he wanted but bending to all of his demands was a little crazy!

Yeah, he might be the hottest graphic artist out there but no one was worth all of the hassle she was going through. She deserved a life outside of these four walls. Taking another glance at her watch, Jazmaine noticed she had been waiting almost forty-five minutes for Mr. Mashiro's assistant to show up and she was done.

If Mr. Kent wanted these contracts finalized it would be done by someone else at the office, but it wouldn't be here. She was finished waiting on these people while they did as they pleased and kept her here for no good reason. She did have other things that had to be dealt with besides this nonsense.

Jazmaine grabbed the two files off the conference room table, along with her cell phone and purse. She was out of here and nothing was going to stop her from leaving this time. If Julie Kim wanted to blow up her cell phone complaining about how she left, she would get the answering machine until tomorrow morning.

Shoving the files inside her purse, Jazmaine dialed Maymi's cell phone number as she stormed around the table. Hopefully, her girlfriend was still up for a couple of drinks and girl's talk. Tatum was out of town of business, so she couldn't call her up and drag her out for nachos and beer. She cursed under her breath when Maymi's voice mail picked up on the other end and she waited to leave a message.

"Hey. Leave me a message and I'll get back to you."

"Maymi, it's me Jazmaine. I'm headed home. Call me if you still want to go out for drinks or you can just come over to my place. I'll fix up some snacks and we can gossip. I got stood up by Mr. Mashiro's assistant, so I'm done waiting for her and dealing with that jerk for the night," She opened the conference room door and then ran into a hard chest on the other side.

"Oh my God," Jazmaine screamed catching her phone before it hit the floor. "You scared the hell out of me." She looked up and her heart literally stopped in her chest at the sight of the man staring down at her.

Her eyes froze on his long, lean form because he was absolutely handsome with his captivating dark eyes. She had never seen anyone who looked like him before in her life. His smooth olive skin stretched over high cheekbones as he smiled at her showing off strikingly white teeth.

She noticed his hair was black and thick styled with a few spiked hairs on the top just enough to give him a bad boy look. She had never looked at a Japanese man before but she couldn't take her eyes off of him. She was completely fascinated by the aura surrounding him.

"I'm sorry. I wasn't expecting you to open the door," he apologized in a slight British accent.

"No, I should have been paying attention to where I was going. I'm Jazmaine Ramey. Can I help you with something Mr.—"

"Mr. Akito Mashiro," he said, shocking her. "I'm sorry I'm late but my plane just arrived about twenty minutes ago from London. I made it here as fast as my driver could get me."

She blinked a couple of times trying to get her thoughts together. Jazmaine crossed her fingers that he hadn't heard the tail end of her conversation on the phone. If Mr. Mashiro had, then all of the hard work she'd put in up to now was ruined and Mr. Kent would lose all of his investments he put into this deal.

"Mr. Mashiro, I wasn't expecting to see you. I thought your assistant Ms. Kim was coming to take care of the final paperwork for our deal," she admitted.

Mr. Mashiro gave her a long, searching look and she started to believe he might have heard her call him a jerk on the phone. "Ms. Kim did her job up to now but I wanted to look at the final paperwork myself. I'm the one who's making this agreement with your boss. I'm the graphic artist, not her. Can you stay and go over it with me?" he asked. "I've a few questions about a couple of things."

The word no was on the tip of her tongue. This guy may be *hot* but he still hadn't done anything but make her life a living hell for the past several months. Jazmaine wanted to tell him where he could go, yet she swallowed it down and smiled instead.

"I'll be glad to help you," she said, stepping back into the conference room. "Mr. Kent and I want to make this transition as easy as possible for you."

Following her inside, Mr. Mashiro flashed her a grin that made her stomach flip flop, but she held it together like a professional. "Please all me Akito. My father is Mr. Mashiro."

"I think I should keep it professional, don't you?"

"So, does that mean I can't call you Jazmaine," he asked in his perfect accent. "It's such a beautiful name."

Baby, you can call me anything you want with that sexy voice of yours.

"Ms. Ramey will be better," Jazmaine answered ignoring the compliment Mr. Mashiro gave her. She took a seat at the table and then pulled the files out of her purse placing them in front of her.

"I'll have to work on getting rid of all of this proper manner for you," Akito said, joining her.

Without commenting to Mr. Mashiro, she watched as he laid a briefcase down and opened it up. He pulled out several files along with one of his graphic novels that he placed on top. Jazmaine was surprised she hadn't noticed the briefcase until now. She had gotten taken by surprise finding him on the other side of the door but she still should have seen a gray metal briefcase in his hand. It wasn't like her to ignore something in plain sight.

Jazmaine got her drifting thoughts under better control as her eyes landed on one of his famous graphic novels. She had seen them before but never had the chance to hold one in her hand.

"Do you mind if I look at your work?" she asked, pointing towards the book..

"Please do," Akito replied, watching as she picked it up.

The novel had a much sturdier feel in her hands than the comic books she was used to holding. No wonder they lasted longer and could be re-read without getting ruined as easily. The colorful designed artwork on the cover stood out to her as well. Akito Mashiro did amazingly beautiful work. No wonder his gifted hands and mind were in such a high demand overseas as well as in the United States.

His work with Manga characters was brilliant with his detail to their distinctive features with large oversized eyes, small noses and a line for a mouth. Some Japanese artists didn't follow this style, but he did and that's what drew her boss to the man sitting across from her.

Jazmaine flipped through the pages before sliding it back across the table. "Your work is really outstanding, the best I have ever seen," she praised. "Mr. Kent is very excited about making you a part of his team over here."

"Ms. Ramey, thank you for the compliment," he told her. Picking up the novel, he placed it back into his briefcase. "I was very impressed by the way you handled my assistant Julie. She can be a bit of a headache to some people, but she informed me how you always kept your cool."

She listened to Mr. Mashiro talk while trying not to get lost in the darkness of his eyes. A man with a good-looking face and a killer accent was always her down fall when it came to dating. Her pickiness could be one of the causes she was thirty-four years old and still single. She'd made up her mind four years ago to stop dating guys who weren't worthy of her.

"Ms. Kim was demanding at times, but I can understand she did it because she only wanted the best for her boss, Mr. Mashiro."

"I really hate being called Mr. Mashiro. I might be a little older than you, but not enough for you to address me so respectfully," he said. "How can we work together with all of this going on? It will make it hard for me to concentrate on my work."

Sitting up straighter in her seat, Jazmaine tried to calm down her racing heart. *Did she actually hear what she thought she just heard?* Was Akito Mashiro just acknowledged that he was going to sign with Kent Publications? What happened to the concerns he wanted to discuss with her less than twenty minutes ago?

"Are you telling me that you're ready to sign with Kent Publications to release the American debut of your Graphic Novels: *Temptation, Wanton, Captive* and *Surrender?*" she asked barely keeping the rising excitement out of her voice.

Working as Mr. Kent's personal assistant in this specialty books industry had been exciting but nothing compared to this moment, if Mr. Mashiro actually put his famous signature on the dotted line.

"Yes," he answered.

"I do have one question, though," Jazmaine admitted. "I thought you had some points in the contracts for us to go over."

Akito's long, tapered fingers pulled down the sleeve of his perfectly tailored dark gray suit as he continued watching her. Honestly, she believed his eyes hadn't ever left hers since they almost collided at the door.

"I did but after speaking with you. I got all of them answered. I believe now your boss's company is the best place for my newest series.

Picking up the folders off the table, he held them out to her. "Here's all of the signed paper work Mr. Kent wanted from me as well as my lawyers. Have him look over everything to make sure it is in order. If he agrees, he can sign and we'll be in business for the next three years."

Jazmaine took the files from Akito while trying to keep cool as possible for two reasons. One, she actually got a multi-million dollar deal under her belt and two, she was extremely attracted to Mr. Mashiro. She hadn't thought about what he looked like; however, she never knew he would be *this* good-looking.

Thank goodness she wouldn't be working with him in close quarters. She wasn't sure if she would be able to control herself around him. After all of the paperwork was taken care of, he would be assigned to a different co-worker who would answer any questions Mr. Mashiro might have about the promotion of his books.

"I will give these to my boss tomorrow and have him look over them. Is there a phone number we can call you directly or should I call Ms. Kim with the final details?"

Leaning across the table, Akito folded his hands causing the sterling silver bracelet on his wrist to bang against the top. "How about you call me personally and then I can invite you to celebrate over drinks?" he flirted, shocking her. She hadn't expected him to ask her out on a date.

As much as her mind was pushing her to accept his surprising offer, Jazmaine knew from experience it was better to keep your business and personal life separate from each other. It helped to keep an unwanted headache out of the workplace.

"I'm sorry, but I can't go out with you. It wouldn't be professional." She gathered up all of the files shoving them into her oversized black purse.

God, she was going to need more than one glass of wine when she got home since she had just turned down a date with a seriously *hot* looking guy.

"Are you sure there isn't anything I can do to change your mind?" Akito asked, standing up.

Jazmaine shook her head. "No, I'm sorry there isn't," she said. "However, it was very nice to finally meet you. I hope your time with Kent Publications will be enjoyable as well as profitable."

"I've already gotten more than I expected," he answered, studying her closely.

She didn't even try to guess what Mr. Mashiro meant. His presence was already weakening her into changing her mind about his invitation to have drinks, so she needed to get out of this closed in room.

"If you're ready to leave, we can walk to the elevator together," Jazmaine suggested going around the table and then heading for the door.

"I would like that." Mr. Mashiro moved away from his seat, walking across the room. He made it to the door and opened it.

"After you," he said, stepping to the side allowing her just enough space to brush past him.

Her body barely missed touching his arm, but she still felt the warmth from his body through his clothing and got a nice whiff of his expensive cologne.

"Thank you," Jazmaine said stepping into the hallway.

"You're more than welcome, Jazmaine."

Stopping in her tracks; she glanced over her shoulder staring at Mr. Mashiro and found him looking straight back at her. "I thought we already agreed not to use our first names."

"No, you suggested it but I never agreed to anything. Let's go. I don't want to keep you any longer than I already have." Placing his hand in the center of her back, Mr. Mashiro spun her back around and led her down the hallway then out the office door towards the elevators.

Jazmaine didn't know what to say but one thing was certain. She would make sure to keep her distance from Akito once he started working here. She could tell he wasn't used to hearing the word no.

He might get his way pretty easily with other people, but he wasn't going to get any special treatment from her. Sure, Mr. Mashiro traveled from the other side of the world to be here, but she still knew trouble when she saw it and he was it with a Capital T.

Chapter Twenty

"Are you serious?" Maymi asked before grabbing a KFC chicken bite out of the container and taking a nibble.

Jazmaine showed up at her front door less than an hour ago with food and a bottle of wine begging her for some advice. Now, they were on her couch with their shoes kicked off eating fattening food and sipping on an aged bottle of liquor.

"I'm not kidding," Jazmaine answered. "He asked me out for drinks and I turned him down. Was I out of my mind? I mean a wealthy, hot, international millionaire wanted to spend time with me and I shot him down in seconds after the words left his mouth. Shit! I should have done a Tatum."

Maymi barely caught herself before she choked on her wine. "No, I wouldn't go that far. Our girl has a wild streak you shouldn't want to copy."

Placing her wine glass down on the table, her friend pulled her legs up to her chest. "Fine, I won't become a carbon copy of Tatum. I'll stick to my words and not go out with Akito. So, enough about me, tell me how are things going with you and Jensen?"

She took another sip of her wine and glanced away looking at the picture of her Nana on the Maplewood stand in her living room. "He asked me out on a date and I said yes. I think he might have been jealous of how fast I became close to his brother Casper."

"It's about time," Jazmaine laughed. "Believe me; it had nothing to with any brother. He wants you. I saw how he was looking at you at the restaurant than night."

Her head swung back in her best friend's direction. She was taken aback by Jazmaine's response. "You aren't surprised, are you?"

"Of course not," she replied, honestly. "Jensen might not want

Sinful next door to his gym, but he definitely wants you. Once you sparked his interest any other common sense he had left went out the door. Have some fun with him, it's not like he'll turn into your everlasting love or anything."

"I don't know if I can," Maymi replied..

"I know you still miss Hudson and he was one of a kind, but it has been over two years since his motorcycle accident. It's okay for you to start dating other men."

Maymi placed her glass down on the table inches from Jazmaine's. "I know I should, but it's still hard. I constantly begged him not to ride without a stupid helmet, but he never listened to me. When I got the news he skidded on a patch of oil on the highway and went over that cliff I almost lost it. He had been such a huge part of me becoming a pastry chef. He was my biggest supporter. How could I even think about being interested in someone who is the polar opposite of Hudson?

"Do you know he was the one who thought of the name Sinful when I told him I wanted to open up my own bakery? He told me biting into one my cookies were like having a sin in his mouth.

"Jensen hates what I do for a living. He might be attracted to me, but it's only hormones or chemistry. The core part of who he is wants me gone from the block. No matter how many dates we go on or unbelievable hot kisses we experience with each other, nothing will *ever* change his first impression of me. It would be for the best if I cancel the date entirely."

Moving her legs, Jazmaine's hand reached out and touched hers. "I guess it's left up to you to make that change happen, isn't it?"

"What if I only want one date and nothing else?" Maymi tossed back.

"I would suggest that you have a kick ass first date and then move on but don't stay hidden behind cream cheese frosting and no bake cookies for the rest of your life," Jazmaine teased.

Smiling, Maymi let go of her friend's hand and slid across the couch then gave her a huge hug. She leaned back and stared into a pair of kind, light brown eyes that reminded her of cinnamon sticks.

"You're too good for me. Thanks for being such a wonderful listening ear," she said. "Do you think you're able to drive or would you rather crash here in the spare bedroom tonight?"

"I need to head home," Jazmaine answered. "Do you have coffee fixed? I think two cups will have me ready to go since I only had two glasses of wine."

"I fixed some this morning before work. Let me get it for you. It will only take a minute." Maymi got up from the couch and went towards the kitchen wondering if Jensen was thinking about their upcoming date like she was.

⁓⁓

"What are you doing here?" Jensen asked the half naked woman standing on his porch. Chloe's outfit was more set for the strip club than a late night visit. He wasn't interested in seeing her tonight or any other day of the week to be truthful.

His mind hadn't been able to think about anything else but Maymi since he got home. She had texted him her address and phone number while he was at work. He held back calling her until he got home because he wanted to hear her voice before he went to bed. He wasn't expecting to deal with this tonight when his doorbell rang.

"I came to see you," Chloe said, touching his bare chest. "Is there a problem with me being here? You used to love my surprises visits."

He removed her cold fingers from his body without even looking at them. "Yes, there is. The last time we talked you told me you were over me because I couldn't give you enough of my time, and I took you at your word."

"Jensen, you know how I can be," she pouted, running her fingers down his arms this time. "Half the time I say something I really don't mean."

Frowning at Chloe, he brushed her hand away from him for a second time and took a step back. "Look, I'm not going to do this with you. It's late and I need to get to bed. So, why don't you go home and do the same thing?" Jensen suggested.

Chloe glared at him as she crossed her arms over her bare stomach. "Who is she?" she demanded.

"I don't know what you are talking about," he said, hoping she would leave so it wouldn't be too late to call Maymi.

"The bitch you're trying to get rid of me for," she shouted, taking a step towards the door. "Is she in there with you? I swear if she is I'll rip the hair out of her head. No whore tries to steal what is mine."

Blocking the door with his body, Jensen touched Chloe gently on her shoulder moving her away from him. She wasn't about to come inside his house. He would never be able to get her to leave.

"You aren't welcomed here anymore," he said. "We are over and have been for a while. Who I date or don't date isn't any of your concern. So, how about you leave before I call the police?"

Moving back, she continued giving him a hateful look. Jensen recalled the fiery temper Chloe used to have but he hadn't seen it in a while. "You're going to regret this Jensen and so is that stupid bitch you are sleeping with. I'll make sure of it," she threatened before storming away him.

He continued standing in the doorway and watching Chloe until she got into her black Corvette and sped off. He wasn't worried about her threats because she did it a lot while they were dating, but never went through with any of them.

Jensen stepped back inside closing the door behind him. For sure now, it was too late for him to call Maymi and tomorrow he was teaching four classes. He wouldn't have a chance to sneak away to see her. Friday would actually be the next time he got to see her. Maymi dared him to do something impressive and that is just what he was going to do.

Chapter Twenty-One

Friday night...

"No, he hasn't showed up yet, Jazmaine," Maymi said, checking her appearance one last time in the mirror. "He still has twenty minutes to get here, so I'm not worried about him not showing up."

"Remember, don't bring up anything negative," Jazmaine told her. "Tonight is about getting you back out there in the dating field. Jensen could be the perfect man to get you back on track."

"He's perfect if you wanted to hire him as your personal trainer, but I'm not so sure about being first date material," she said.

"Stop being such a negative Jane. Just live in the moment. If I can't date a hot, sexy man you might as well do it for the both of us," her friend teased.

"How does it feel to finally have the aloof Mr. Mashiro working at your business?" Maymi asked, wanting to get the conversation off her for a few minutes.

"I got caught with him in the elevator this morning." Jazmaine sighed. "He asked me out on a date for tomorrow night but I told him that I already had plans."

"Jazmaine, you made him think you were going out with another man," she scolded walking away from the mirror. Maymi picked up her purse off the bed and left the bedroom. "You could have invited him to the party tomorrow night. Honestly, I'm dying to meet the man who has gotten you so turned around after only one meeting."

Inside the living room, Maymi went over to her black couch and sat down. She was glad she had Jazmaine on the phone. It would take her mind off worrying if Jensen was going to show up tonight.

"No, it wouldn't have been a good idea," she disagreed. "I told you that I'm not going to ever have an office romance. I've seen how bad they can go at previous jobs and swore that wouldn't ever be me. Besides, tonight is about you anyway and how fast you can strip Jensen out of his clothes."

"Jazmaine!" Maymi gasped, shocked. "I wasn't even thinking about seeing him naked. All I'm doing is going out on one date and nothing else is going to happen. I can promise you that."

"Sure, it won't if you don't let him kiss you."

"I don't have any plans for that to happen," Maymi answered.

Jazmaine giggled. "Keep lying to yourself. I know you and despite what might be coming out of your mouth, you want a taste of Mr. Lowe. Admit it and then get you some. It's only sex and not a walk down the aisle."

Maymi tried not to laugh, but she couldn't stop it from escaping. "Okay, enough wine for you. Put down the glass and get yourself something to eat. I don't want you hung over for the party tomorrow night."

"I'm not going to even ask how you knew I was drinking. However, I will order something from that Thai place a few blocks from here and then I'll crawl into bed. I think they're having a Syfy movie marathon tonight. I'll watch some of those before I fall asleep," Jazmaine said before hanging up.

Sometimes she wondered how she got such a crazy best friend, but Maymi knew one thing for sure. She wouldn't trade Jazmaine or Tatum for anything in the world. Picking up her purse off the couch, she slid her cell phone inside as the buzzer went off. She took a quick glance at the clock on the table noticing Jensen was twenty minutes early.

She got up from the couch and made her way over to the intercom, pressing the button with her finger. "Yes, who is it?"

"It's me, Jensen. Buzz me up."

"You're early. What if I'm not ready yet?" she asked.

"Still buzz me up and I can help you with any button or zipper you're having a problem with. I'm very good with my hands."

"God, is this how you're going to be all night," Maymi teased.

"Babe, if you just ring me up already I can give you a sneak preview of things to come," Jensen answered.

"Fine, come on up." Maymi pressed the button to let Jensen upstairs. A few minutes later there was a knock on her door.

Walking over to it, she blew out a deep breath hoping tonight didn't turn into a total disaster. She placed her hand on the doorknob, turned it and then opened it. Her eyes widened at the sight of Jensen standing there in front of her. She thought he might look nice in a suit, but she never expected that he would look anything like *this*.

He stood there, tall, handsome, in a perfectly tailored dark suit with a white shirt underneath opened at the throat. The fabric molded his muscles to perfection bringing her wandering eyes to his narrow hips and long legs. Even his dark hair looked like he'd gotten it cut a little since she had last seen him a few days ago. Jensen was a totally different man than she was used to seeing at the gym.

"You look very handsome," she said, taking the rose he brought from behind his back.

"You're breathtaking," Jensen whispered as he bent down to brush a kiss against her cheek.

She noticed how his eyes lingered on the cleavage exposed by her red, form fitting dress that stopped right above her knees. It was a spur of the moment purchase a few months ago that she had shoved to the back of her closet.

"If my breasts could talk, from the way you're staring at them, they would thank you for your interests in them," she teased, making Jensen's bedroom brown eyes dart back up to hers.

"Sorry, I couldn't help myself," he apologized, standing back up to his full height.

"Don't worry about it. Would you like to come inside while I grab my things?" She stepped back waving Jensen into her apartment then closed the door.

"I wasn't expecting you to live in a loft," he said, walking past her.

Maymi took another sniff of her rose before walking around him. She noticed how he was glancing at some of the art work and pictures from her baking competitions hanging on the walls.

"I decided to skip buying a house and put that money into Sinful. Tatum's family owns the building, so I get a very good deal on the rent." Maymi placed the rose in a glass of water she had left on the table earlier then grabbed her purse and coat off the couch.

"Here let me help you with your coat." Jensen walked over to her and took it from her then held it while she slipped it on.

"Did I tell you how good you smell?" he whispered by her ear.

She tried not to moan as Jensen's warm breath brushed against her skin. They hadn't even made it out of the door yet and she was dying for him to kiss her already.

Get a hold of yourself girl. Calm down. It's only a date.

"No, you haven't," she answered, spinning around she looked up into his eyes.

"Well, you do."

"Thank you. It's a new fragrance I bought the other day."

"You're welcome, sweetheart. How about we get going?" he suggested. "I don't want us to be late for our reservations."

"Where are we going?" Maymi asked as she walked towards the door with Jensen at her side.

"It's a surprise." Reaching past her, he opened the door and held it while she went out into the hallway.

Outside, Maymi quickly locked the door while Jensen stood next to her. He didn't say a word, but she could feel his dark eyes as they roamed up and down the length of her body. His interest in her made her feel sexy and very womanly which proved she had done an excellent job at getting ready.

"Aren't you going to give me a hint?" she asked as she moved away from the door.

"Let's just say you're going to have stars in your eyes," he answered pressing the button.

Maymi peeked at him from the corner of her eye wondering what he had planned for their date. She hadn't been this curious by a comment in forever.

Time would tell if Jensen could actually keep his word or if he was only full of empty promises, she thought as the elevator stopped in front of them and opened up.

Chapter Twenty-Two

"Oh my God Jensen, this place is unbelievable," Maymi praised as he pulled her chair out for her.

The Botanic Gardens was one of the most exclusive buildings in town because the outside part of the restaurant was surrounded by a glass enclosure almost like a dome. It seemed like millions of stars were in the sky shining down of them.

The design was set up to enable customers to see the flower garden which looked like a perfect scene from the rain forest. Fresh flowers were one of her favorite things in the world; she bought them anytime she had the extra money to spend on them.

"I'm so glad you like it," Jensen said, taking a seat in front of her. "I thought you might like the view. I loved learning about the stars as a kid with my dad, so I thought this would be a place for both of us to enjoy our first date."

Turning away from the garden, Maymi looked at Jensen. "I find it very hard to believe you were looking through a telescope trying to find the legendary Big Dipper," she teased.

He arched an eyebrow. "I'll have you know that I won several science fairs when I was in school. I was almost considered a science nerd."

"You weren't ever a nerd."

"Oh, you would be surprised. I didn't always have this body and my winning charm."

"I find that very hard to believe," Maymi admitted, smiling at Jensen. "Well. Maybe not about the charm, but you've gotten better since I first met you. You don't come off as intimidating or rude."

"Let me apologize for that," he said, cutting her off. "I shouldn't have spoken to you like I did. I want us to get that experience behind us for good."

"So, do I," Maymi admitted.

※

Sitting across the table from Maymi, Jensen couldn't get over how stunning she truly looked tonight. Her dark hair was finally out of the familiar ponytail and the ends brushed the top of her shoulders drawing his eyes to her smooth skin that looked like dark chocolate. Earlier, he had fought the need to brush his lips across the side of her neck when he pulled out her chair earlier.

She looked almost too breathtaking to even bring out for their date with the way the firecracker red dress hugged all of her womanly curves. Most of his dates where so slender that their bodies never filled out a dress the way Maymi's was doing tonight.

His cock was so hard right now that it was painful to sit across from her and only be able to look at her delicious body. He wanted to hold, touch and without a doubt make love to her, but he had to take things slowly with her.

The main objective was to get through this date without anything coming up and get a second lined up as soon as possible. He knew going out once with her wasn't going to be enough for him.

Reaching for the glass of water the waiter had placed there earlier, Jensen practically drained it in one swallow. He couldn't afford to drink anything strong at the moment. His self-control was hanging on by a thread and after two months without sex, being around Maymi was a test he wasn't prepared for.

"Jensen, are you alright?" Maymi asked, her soft voice filled with genuine concern.

He placed the glass back down and gave her a smile. "Yes, I'm fine. How about you tell me why you decided to become a pastry chef? It just seems like a very specific field to aspire for at such a young age."

"I just turned twenty-eight the beginning of this year, so I don't know about the young part," she sighed.

"Sweetheart, I'm thirty-seven, so you're young to me. Now, tell me how you got this dream."

Maymi gazed at him as a tiny smile started forming at the corner of her full, perfect lips. "It was my Nana. She loved baking things from scratch. I used to watch her all of the time, but never really got into it until after my mother's suicide when I was a little girl."

"God, I'm so sorry," he cut in, meaning it. Jensen couldn't believe Maymi had been through something so traumatic.

"I had just turned nine years old. My mama always had this sadness about her, but we never thought she would take her own life. My dad had the hardest time accepting it, but he pulled himself together for my two older brothers.

"Well, I started spending most of my time after school or counseling at my Nana's house. My mama's mother had been an outstanding cook and baker. I don't think here wasn't anything she couldn't turn into a masterpiece."

"Sounds like you loved her a lot," Jensen commented, but he noticed how Maymi didn't bring up her father again.

"I did and when she died five years ago, it broke my heart for a very long time. It took me a while to get over saying goodbye to her and I don't think I could if it hadn't been for Hudson."

Who in the hell was Hudson?

Jensen wanted to ask, but the hurt in Maymi's voice made him realize that this date was going down the wrong road. He wanted her in the present with him and not in the past.

"How about we change gears and order something to eat?" he suggested. "After we're finished how about we take a walk around the rest of the gardens?"

Maymi's beautiful face lit up with excitement. "Are you sure that we can? I thought some parts were off limits to the public."

"I'm friends with someone over the place. He gave me the all go to give my date the complete tour if she wanted it."

The sadness left her eyes as she perked up in her seat. The happiness in her expression now brought a grin to his face. He wasn't used to doing something so small for any of his dates, but getting such a huge reward in return.

"I can tell you're excited."

"Of course. The Botanic Gardens' is famous for its award-winning desserts," she gushed. "I mean I've heard one bite will send you to heaven and back."

He looked into Maymi's dark eyes and felt a falling sensation. He saw the passion she had there and secretly wondered what else he could do to keep it there for the rest of the night.

"Would you rather we have the tour first and then eat?" Jensen suggested.

She shook her head. "I adore a mouth-watering dessert, but I've heard the Beef Wellington here is also to die for, so I'll start that first and see where we can go after it."

"Alright, let's get some food into you."

Raising his hand, Jensen waved a waiter hovering in the shadows watching them over to the table. He paid the extra money for the guy to be here and not seen until he was ready. His date with Maymi was about him impressing her without any interruptions from the waiter or his flirtatious brother.

After the waiter stopped staring at Maymi's breasts long enough to finally take their orders and then left them alone, he leaned across the table and grabbed her hand.

"Thank you for accepting my dinner invitation."

"How could I not when you promised to blow my mind like no other man has before?" she reminded him.

"Did I keep my promise?"

Maymi looked away from him glancing around the room for a few minutes then her gaze landed back in his direction. "You kept your promise and did so much more. I'm very impressed."

Her admission pleased him. "Let's see if I can keep it up until I take you back home after our date."

Chapter Twenty-Three

Standing in the semi-dark hallway after giving Maymi a tour of The Botanic Gardens like he had promised her, Jensen stared down into Maymi's face wondering if she felt the same shift in the air surrounding them. All during dinner and the tour they had been dancing around it. He had taken her all over the place until they finally found their way back here. He knew he wouldn't be able to leave this spot without kissing her.

Neither one of them wanted to make the first move, but he had given in because he couldn't hold back anymore. The memory of how sweet her lips had tasted were *too* powerful to forget.

He moved closer and closer until her back touched the wall only a few feet from the dining room where they just had dinner. He knew he should take her home, but he couldn't leave without doing this or the drive back to her place would be hell on his body. He needed something to tide him over until he dropped her off and then drove back to his place.

Jensen placed a hand on Maymi's hips and drew her to his throbbing body. Maymi trembled, but she didn't move away or push him back which was a good sign in his opinion.

"I need to kiss you," he admitted, brushing his lips across her mouth.

"Is that really a good idea," she asked, softly. "I mean every time we kiss it seems to mess with our ability to think rationally."

"Don't you like not knowing what's coming next?" Jensen asked not backing down.

She lifted her head. "Too much of the unknown can get a girl into trouble and I try to stay out of that as much as possible."

Maymi's sweet sexiness was already pushing him over the brink towards the land of no return, so why shouldn't he take her along for the ride?

He gently traced the side of her mouth with his tongue. This was their first kiss not done out of anger or the need to prove something to the other person and he wanted it to be done right...almost perfect so she would relive it after their date was over.

Jensen continued teasing the corner of her lips. The faint taste of chocolate and caramel still lingered there from the dessert she had eaten after dinner.

She moaned softly and he took the opportunity to touch the tip of his tongue to hers before sneaking it the rest of the way inside. With his willpower barely intact, he slid his hands down the side of her waist and stopped them as her hips brushed his erection against her stomach.

He devoured Maymi's lips taking everything she offered while giving back something of his own. The feel and taste of her consumed him like a burning fire. She had him spinning out of control.

Instead of moving away, she pressed closer running her fingers through his hair. He felt her hard nipples against his chest as he sucked her tongue into his mouth. Easing his hand around her body, he moved her away from the wall so he could hold her rounded ass in the palm of his hands, deepening their kiss even more.

Mewling, she eased her arms around his shoulders. Maymi didn't know how much she was pushing him to his breaking point out in a public place. His cock was aching to be inside of her sweet, tight body. He grabbed her hair gently pulling it to separate their mouths with a soft sucking sound.

He stared down into her upturned face and saw the desire he wanted shining there. God, why did he get dinner here instead of having it at his place? He couldn't make love to her here. They could only go so far in front of other people. He might not be able to see them, but he knew the staff was standing somewhere looking at them.

"Sweetheart, I want you but we can't get carried away here. We need some privacy. How about we go back to my house since I live closer than you do?" he suggested.

The desire-filled look slowly started clearing from her eyes. "Go back to your house," she whispered, staring at him blankly.

"Yes, go back to my place so we can finish what we had going on here," he said. Taking his thumb, he ran it over her swollen bottom lip. "Like I said, I don't live far from here. We can be back at my house in less than forty minutes."

Touching his wrist, she moved his hand away. "I can't go back to your house. I'm sorry I let the kiss get carried away."

Maymi tried to move around his body, but he grabbed her by the waist and backed her against the wall holding her there with his body. He grabbed her by the chin forcing her to look him in the eye.

Jensen saw how her earlier look had been replaced by one of mistrust. He wanted to know what changed between them so quickly. She had been into it as much as him, but now she was a totally different person.

"Sweetheart, what happened? Did I do something wrong?"

She shook her head. "No, it's me. I'm just not ready for more than this first date yet. Can you please take me home?"

He wanted to push further and find out why she had withdrawn from him, but he wouldn't do it. He actually had a better time with her tonight than he thought he would. If he wanted a second date with her, he had to respect her wishes.

"Okay, I'll take you home. It's getting late and I don't want you to be late for work tomorrow, but I have one more thing to ask you before we leave." Lowering his head, Jensen brushed his lips along her smooth neck.

"Oh, you aren't playing fair," she whispered. "I thought I told you no sex."

"Baby, this isn't sex. We are making out which to my disappointment means our clothes will stay on tonight."

Maymi touched his shoulder and he moved back from her. Staring down into her eyes, he saw a tiny bit of uncertainty there working its way into her dark brown depths.

"Are you playing games with me?" she asked, her expression confused. "I don't want to be used in any way, shape or form.

He sucked in a breath wondering if he would be able to erase Maymi's first impression of him away forever. She did have a memory like a steel trap. It might be excellent for keeping track of recipes, but it was a death sentence for a blooming relationship. Tonight's date wouldn't be over for him until he left her thinking about something else altogether.

"Haven't you ever made a split second decision and then regretted it later," Jensen asked, running his hands up and down Maymi's sides.

"Of course, I have," she admitted, honestly. "Who hasn't in their life? It's a part of growing up and becoming who you are. A person can't grow unless they learn from their mistakes and then find the strength to move on."

He sighed then brushed the back of his hand along the side of her cheek. "How about you try that with me? If I'm not mistaken, I think we had a pretty good time over dinner. I learned a lot more about you and vice versa. However, you are still somewhat of a mystery to me. I want to figure you out, but I can't do it if you don't give me the opening to do—"

Maymi pressed a finger against his lips. "You're right," she admitted. "I'm bringing extra baggage on this date and I shouldn't have. I had a great time and I want to end it on the high note it started on."

Taking the tip of his tongue, Jensen licked Maymi's finger. She moaned softly before easing it away from his mouth. "You are *so* bad."

"I know I am which means you're going to agree to have dinner with me again tomorrow night at my place. I want to have you all to myself next time."

"I'm sorry, I can't," she answered very quickly without missing a beat.

Chapter Twenty-Four

Growling in frustration, Jensen pushed his body away from Maymi's storming down the hallway putting some distance between them. He raked his fingers through his hair and slowly counted to ten.

Damn it! Nothing was going as he had hoped it work.

"You warned me about playing games with you, so why are you doing it to me?" he demanded.

"Jensen, I'm not doing anything to you," Maymi denied. "If you had let me finish, I would have told you I'm throwing a small party tomorrow night for one of my girlfriends. She just landed a big client for her boss. Would you like to come? You can even bring Casper. I think we'll have a great time together."

She moved around him and stared up into his face. "So, how about it? Do you want to celebrate with me and my friends and eat a piece of carrot cake? I might even make some finger food to go with it."

"Hell, I'm good," Jensen bragged as the anger left his body. "After one date you're ready to introduce me to your girlfriends. I would love to meet them. Are they the same two I saw with you at the restaurant that night?"

She nodded. "Yes, Jazmaine and Tatum. We've been friends since I moved here from Atlanta. We do everything together, but all of us have been so busy lately that we haven't had the time to do anything."

Maymi wanted him to meet her friends so soon. He had dated Chloe for months and never was in the same room with one woman who liked her. None of them would have claimed Chloe as their friend, because she wasn't a nice person.

Her willingness to do this showed him she was open to them moving further than the one date.

"I'll be there and I guess I can bring Casper along with me. However, I'll warn him to be on his best behavior. He can get a little out of hand sometimes around beautiful women."

"Don't you dare," Maymi scolded. "Casper is Casper. Besides, he isn't the one I want my girlfriends to meet. You are."

Looking into Maymi's eyes, Jensen saw the truth staring back at him. She was interested in seeing where things could go between them by inviting him to her party. He wouldn't ruin it by allowing his unfound jealously of Casper to show its ugly head.

"I will be there with Casper. What time is the party?"

"Seven o'clock," she answered.

"How about I come over earlier and I'll help you bake something. I mean there's nothing more romantic than two people working together in the kitchen side by side." The idea of watching Maymi bake seemed a lot more inviting this time then when he first saw her working at Sinful.

"You are too much, Jensen." Maymi was barely able to keep the laughter from her voice as she touched him on the arm. "The two of us inside the kitchen together working wouldn't work. I think it would be better if you showed up at the designated time. I do my best work alone."

Grabbing her by the hips, he yanked Maymi to his body, grinding his erection against her. "I'll have to disagree with you. I think some events are better with a partner."

She pressed closer, raking her fingers through his hair. "I agree with you, but having you inside my kitchen isn't one of those things, sweetheart." Maymi placed her hands on his chest and pushed him back.

"I think it's time for me to be heading home. I need to be at Sinful pretty early. I need to make some patty cakes and chocolate delights."

He gave Maymi a quick kiss. "I think it's way too early for our date to end, but I understand about your job so I'll take you home. I don't want you missing out on any extra rest."

Placing his hand under her elbow, he led Maymi back through the hallway of The Botanic Gardens towards the front door. From the corner of his eye, he watched how she continued looking at everything like it was as incredible as when she saw it the first time.

He never had a date before appreciate something so small. This restaurant was pricey, but not as expensive as some of the places Chloe whined about visiting until he took her just to shut her up about it.

Jensen continued ushering Maymi down the hallway until they went down the circular steps then out the door to his car. He opened the passenger door to the black Lexus and waited while Maymi slipped inside giving him a peek of a smooth, toned brown thigh.

His cock hardened inside his slacks at the captivating sight. Jensen pressed his palm against the door so he wouldn't reach out and touch the silkiness of her skin. He stole one last look at his stunning date then closed the door and walked around to the driver's side.

Jensen got inside closing the door behind him. The interior of the car seemed more intimate than before after the hot kiss he'd shared with Maymi. He wouldn't be able to get it out of his mind.

"Jensen, are you okay?" Maymi asked, touching him on the leg.

Sighing, he looked over at her as he laid his hand on top of hers running his thumb over the back. "Yes, I'm fine. I was just thinking."

"Anything I should know about?" she asked.

"No, sweetheart," he answered. "There is nothing you should be worried about. I was only thinking. Let me get you home, so you can make those calorie packed treats of yours to entice my members." Removing his hand from Maymi, Jensen started the car and drove off.

"Would you like to come in for a drink?" Maymi asked, standing in the open doorway of her apartment with an almost hopeful glint in her eyes.

If he came inside right now with the way he felt, Jensen knew that he wouldn't be drinking coffee or anything else with Maymi. They both would be tearing off clothes and be naked on her couch having sex.

He was barely holding on to his hunger to have her nipples inside of his mouth. They had been poking through the fabric of her dress for most of the night *tempting...taunting* him to do something about them.

"No, I don't think it would be a good idea," he finally answered.

"I understand," she said. "I don't know why I even asked you. I completely agree it wouldn't be a good idea for either one of us."

Bending his head, he brushed his mouth across her cheek. He

was entranced by the soft brown of her eyes, but he took a step back to clear his mind. She ran her tongue over her bottom lip. Several thoughts raced through his head about spending time in her apartment using that mouth for other things.

"God, I need to get out of here before I do something that could ruin the wonderful night we just had." He took a step away from Maymi trying to cool down his body.

"Okay, I understand. I think you're right. We might need to end our date here at the door. Goodnight, Jensen."

"Goodnight, Maymi." He turned then started walking away, but he only made it a few steps before spinning back around and grabbing Maymi by the elbow. He pivoted her back around to face him. His mouth captured hers cutting off any protest she might have.

His cock grew even harder as he pressed her back against the wall. Jensen felt himself getting further lost in her long, sweet, accepting kisses and if he didn't stop now there would be *no* going back in a few minutes. He couldn't let that happen with them. He gave her a few more kisses then backed away from the delicious temptation of her full lips.

"Enough, I'm leaving now. I already have a long, cold shower in my future. I probably will at least have to stay in there until I can't stand it."

Holding up his hand, he shook his head at Maymi when she took a step towards him. Jensen took another huge step back and continued doing the same thing until he could no longer reach out and touch her.

"I'll see you tomorrow night?" Maymi asked stepping inside of her apartment.

"You better believe you will," he answered right as she closed the door gently in his face.

Standing in the middle of the hallway, Jensen stared at the closed door for a few minutes. Maymi's personality and wonderful sense of humor impressed him tonight. She hadn't asked him too many questions but he wasn't worried. She was very inquisitive, so it would only be a matter of time before she had some questions of her own. Jensen slid his hands into the pockets of his slacks and then moved in the direction of the elevator happier than he had been in a very long time.

He liked the idea of looking forward to another date with Maymi and seeing where it would take them. He wasn't usually fond of not having an agenda about the future, but this was a rare time he wasn't going to plan everything out every single detail. Sometimes the unknown could be a lot sexier than he was giving it credit for.

Chapter Twenty-Five

"Are you actually going to stand there icing cupcakes like we aren't standing in front of you dying to hear about your date last night?" Tatum asked, placing her hands on her hips.

"Yeah, I mean I was up waiting for a phone call that never came. I'm hurt," Jazmaine chimed in, glaring at her.

Placing the pastry bag down on the counter, Maymi wiped her hands on a towel before she reached for the sprinkles. "There isn't anything to tell," she said, shaking the colorful sugar over the chocolate icing. "Jensen took me to the Botanic Gardens for dinner and then gave me a quick tour of the place. After that he drove me home then walked me to the door and that's it."

Picking up the cupcakes, she stepped around the two nosey friends and went through the door into the bakery. She didn't know what they wanted to hear, but she wasn't about to tell them anything more than she had.

Some of her date last night had to stay with her because it wasn't any of their business to know that she almost slept with Jensen. God, they would never let her hear the last of it.

"Maymi Raven Monroe, don't you dare walk away from us. You know that I'm going to keep asking until I get what I want."

Rolling her eyes, she twirled around and found Tatum staring at her.

"You haven't been out on a date in forever and a day. How can you give us the Cliff Notes version with the sexiest man alive, Jensen. Did you really not kiss him or at least plan a second date?"

"Well, maybe we did share a kiss or two," she admitted.

"Did he get to second base?"

"Jazmaine!" Maymi gasped staring at the woman standing next

to Tatum. "I'm not going into details with you."

Tatum's eyes moved away from her over to Jazmaine. "I know one thing didn't happen and that was a home run because our girl might love this bakery, but not enough to leave handsome Jensen alone in her bed. Besides, she's just having a little fun for the moment. She isn't about to fall in love with the guy."

"Okay, enough," Maymi sighed. "My sex life, or lack of it, isn't the concern of either one of you. How about you get out of here, so I can finish up stocking up the desserts before Olivia comes in? She was nice enough to close the bakery for me so I can start decorating for the party tonight. I need to make a few stops before I head home and get everything ready for tonight."

"Fine, Miss Spoilsport. I'm leaving," Jazmaine said. "I need to finish up something at the office anyway. Mr. Mashiro is still trying to get me to go out with him. It's getting harder and harder to turn him down."

"I saw him giving a press conference about joining Kent Publications. I swear if his exotic face wasn't a turn-on, his voice would do it for me in a hot second. Is there something seriously wrong with your head? Why aren't you saying yes?" Tatum asked.

Maymi wanted to admit she had wondered the same thing more than once. Mr. Mashiro was a very attractive man, so why wasn't Jazmaine interested in going out on at least one date with him. She wasn't buying her excuse about office romances.

"I've told you why, because it wouldn't be very professional for me to date a client. I love my job and dating a wealthy client wouldn't look good for me. I can't say how many work relations I've seen go downhill at my job, and when it's over the woman is the one out looking for a new 9 to 5."

"They aren't you. You can't turn down Mr. Mashiro because of them," Maymi pointed out.

"Look, I can't stay any longer. I need to go, "Jazmaine said, walking past Tatum and heading for the door. "I'll be at your house a little before seven."

Maymi watched as Jazmaine rushed out the door without looking back in their direction. Jazmaine was hiding something from them. There was another reason why she was turning Mr. Mashiro down for a date and she would get to the bottom of it before long. Tatum might be good at keeping secrets from her, but Jazmaine wasn't.

"I better go and make sure she's okay," Tatum said, rushing by her and out of the building.

She would have liked to go and check on them, but she still had a few more things to do before she could leave. Olivia would be here in less than an hour and she wanted to be ready. Heading back to the kitchen, she was halfway here when her cell phone rang. She took it out of her apron pocket and smiled when she noticed the name on the caller ID.

"Hi," she said, answering the phone.

"Hi, yourself," Jensen's rich voice whispered into her ear. "How are you doing this morning? Did you sleep good last night? I know I had a very hard time because I kept replaying our kiss in my head."

"I was out as soon as my head hit the pillow," she answered. "I wanted to tell you that I had an excellent time last night. I loved eating out underneath the stars inside the dome. I wasn't expecting you to do something so romantic or creative for me."

Stopping at the end of the counter, Maymi stared out the window watching as Olivia's car pulled up at the curb. She liked how she always kept her word and showed up on time for work. She was becoming an invaluable part of Sinful.

"Babe, there's a lot about me you don't know. However, I would love to show you some more if you're up to it," he flirted.

"Are you asking me out for another date that doesn't include the party tonight?" Maymi asked, trying to keep the enthusiasm out of her voice. "I mean we're both so busy. I can't promise I've the extra time to spend with you. Do you think you'll be able to top yourself?"

The long pause on the other end of the phone made her nervous. She waved at Olivia as she walked through the front door. She wondered what Jensen was thinking.

"Oh, what, no answer?" she teased, trying to get him back into the conversation.

"Darling, I have an answer for you. I can top last night's dinner, but why should I tell you what it is when you aren't giving me an answer to my question?"

From the corner of her eye, Maymi noticed Olivia standing at the side munching on a cookie while eavesdropping on her conversation. She wasn't going to be able to give Jensen a response without

Olivia teasing her about it later.

"Fine, I'd love to go another date with you, Jensen. Honestly, I was looking forward to seeing you tonight at the party. I think you'll have a good time with my friends."

A deep masculine voice chuckled in her ear sending a tingling sensation straight to her pussy. God, Jensen was making her realize how long it had been since she'd made love to a man.

Would he be the one able to get rid of her dry spell?

Without a single doubt in her mind, she knew Jensen would have the keen ability to make her body sing with pleasure. Just the size of his hands had her wishing they had touched her more during dinner, but he was a perfect gentleman and left her at her front door with only a good night kiss.

"I know that took a lot on your part to admit that you wanted me," he exclaimed.

Maymi nodded then stopped when she realized Jensen couldn't see her. "Yes, it did. Don't make me regret telling you the truth."

"Oh, you won't baby. I have some excellent plans for us. I hate to cut this phone call short, but my class starts in a few minutes so I probably won't see you until tonight."

"Alright," Maymi answered. "Don't forget to bring Casper."

Jensen sighed on the other end of the phone. "I won't forget my little brother. He'll be there unless he has other plans. Casper is never without a date, but I'll make sure he understands that she isn't invited."

"Oh, I didn't know Casper was seeing anyone. I was hoping—"

"What were you hoping for?" Jensen cut in with a little heat in his voice. "Is there another reason that you asked me to bring my brother?"

She heard the hint of anger and Maymi wasn't about to end their pleasant conversation on an argument. "It was nothing. Forget I even brought it up. I'll see both of you tonight at seven. Bye Jensen." Maymi hung up the phone before he could toss another question at her.

She hated to even admit this to herself, but she was truly looking forward to seeing Jensen tonight at her place with everyone else.

After the kiss they shared, it might be a good idea for them to be around other people this time. Since Jensen's kisses were becoming more and more seductive to her wavering senses., they were leading her down a slippery slope she wasn't ready for.

All she was trying to do was have some fun and do a little harmless flirting on her date, but something happened that surprised her. Jensen showed her another side of him. The romantic, carefree Jensen wasn't anything like the demanding bully who had barged into her business.

The sound of fingers snapping in front of her face jolted Maymi back from her inner thoughts. Turning her head, she found Olivia standing not five feet from her with a huge grin on her face.

"Care to tell me what has put that look in your eyes and that tiny smile on your face?" she asked. "Does it have anything to do with your date with the very attractive man next door?"

Smothering a groan, Maymi stepped back. "Alright, I did go out with Jensen last night, but you already knew I had plans with him.. I really had a good time. "

Olivia's eye rose in amazement. "Did you think you actually wouldn't?" she questioned. "I mean every time the two of you are in the same room, everyone and everything else fades to the background as the sparks begin to fly. I'm surprised it took him this long before he asked you out on a date."

"We weren't....I mean I wasn't *that* obvious," she denied. "I thought I hid my fascination for him pretty well."

Her employee made a *tsking* sound with her tongue. "If you believe that, you need to get away from those hot ovens even more. The sexual pull between the two of you almost made me feel like a Peeping Tom anytime I was around. However, I want you to remember something. Safe sex is always the best sex."

"Olivia," she gasped, shocked.

"Hey, I might be old enough to be your mother, but I do remember the days I was driven by explosive chemistry. It was so hard to say no, when all I wanted to do was strip him naked."

Maymi had never felt so embarrassed in her life. She was actually getting sex advice from Olivia. She wasn't some doe-eyed virgin. She knew about sex and what do to.

"Jensen and I are only in the getting to know stage. At any moment, he could say something about Sinful and we will be at each other's throats again. Don't read more into one date than there was."

The words coming out of her mouth sounded so good. She only wished that she believed the half of it herself. The idea of making love with Jensen had entered her mind more than once since she met him. She had to get out of here before Olivia made her tell more than she wanted to.

"You know what, since you're here, I think I can head on out." Maymi walked away from Olivia and grabbed her purse from behind the counter. "Everything you need should be already in the cases. If you get any kind of custom cakes orders, tell them I'll have to call them back."

Olivia nodded as she walked past her. "I know. Don't worry. Have fun getting set up for Jazmaine's party. Sinful will be taken care of just the way you want it."

"I know. Bye," Maymi said, heading out the door.

❧❦

Walking around the side of the building, Maymi was halfway to her car when she spotted a very handsome man coming out of Fitness 24's doors making a beeline for her. Her eyes drank up the sight of Jensen wearing khaki pants and a white polo shirt with Fitness 24 embroidered across the left side on his upper chest.

He stopped only a few feet in front of her. "Were you trying to sneak away without telling me goodbye? I didn't think you would do something like that to me."

"No, I was leaving, no sneaking about it at all. Olivia is here now. I'm leaving so I can pick up a few more things before the party."

"I was thinking once the party was over, I could stay and help you clean up afterwards."

She was enthralled by what she saw, but she couldn't fall for it. She had to see how he interacted with her friends first. Tatum and Jazmaine were a huge part of her life. If he didn't like them then there wouldn't be a third date.

"What has you thinking so hard you have this frown now?" he asked, tracing her forehead with his index finger.

"I was wondering how you're going to get along with my girlfriends," she replied honestly. "They're both very opinionated and won't bite their tongues about anything."

For a moment, he studied her intently. His eyes seemed to be trying to get into her head like he was trying to make sure she wasn't leaving anything out. She had never experienced the look before from any other man, not even Hudson.

"I hope your friends get along with me too. However, if they don't I'm not going worry about it. You're the woman I'm interested in getting to know better, not them."

She found an immense satisfaction in Jensen's words. He was telling her directly what he wanted so there wouldn't be any confusion between them. She couldn't resist touching his face loving how his slight five o'clock shadow brushed across her fingertips.

"You sure do know how to make a woman forget her bad first impression of you."

"Maymi, I've a way of making a woman forget a lot of things," he whispered, lowering his head towards her until his sensual mouth was only inches away.

"You're doing a very good job," she answered, softly staring up into his eyes.

"Let me see if I can do even better for you," he said right before kissing her.

He slipped his tongue inside of her mouth as his body pressed against hers. Maymi whimpered softly wrapping her arms around Jensen's strong shoulders. He groaned against hers lips pressing the bulge in his pants against her stomach.

She whimpered, clinging to him, wanting more than either one of them was getting at the moment. No, she had to fight this off and get herself together before she lost control completely.

"Shit, you taste so good," Jensen moaned against her mouth. "I could keep you here for another hour."

Placing her hands on his chest, Maymi eased Jensen away from her while she still had the strength to do it. "We have to stop."

"Why are you always pushing me to the point of no return?" Jensen asked, running his hands up and down her arms. "You're giving me something that I have never had before."

"What is it? What have I given you that no other woman has done before me?"

"A taste for chocolate," Jensen said before reclaiming her mouth with his.

She stopped fighting trying to be the leader in whatever was happening between her and Jensen. Instead, she gave up and allowed herself to get lost in how *good* his firm lips felt brushing over hers again.

∽∾

As Maymi and Jensen got lost in each other's arms and their hot exploring kiss, neither one of them noticed the pair of hate-filled eyes staring at them from the doorway at Fitness 24. Anger rushed through the person as a plot formed at how to get even with Jensen. He wasn't going to get away with kissing her not now...not ever.

Chapter Twenty-Six

Several hours later after leaving work, Maymi hurried around her apartment checking every single detail of her party to make sure it was relaxed and comfortable. She hadn't wanted to overdo anything because Jazmaine wasn't into anything too flashy.. All of the finger foods were out and ready to be eaten as soon as all of the guests arrived. In addition, the triple layer carrot cake Jazmaine wanted was in the refrigerator. It had taken her a little longer to get it done than usual because of Jensen.

God, just one more kiss from that mouth of his and she was a step away from losing her mind or giving in to what he was offering her. She couldn't afford to allow herself to get lost in him tonight with her girlfriends and his brother around. They were already bad enough when they were alone, they would have to get it together around other people.

Her best friends needed to make their own opinion of Jensen without her getting involved. His new found interest in her appeared genuine enough, but she still wondered if he was still plotting something behind her back.

Stop it, her mind scolded.

She had a way of hanging on to everything when she should be living in the moment and having fun. She would give Jensen as much as he gave her. *Nothing more...nothing less.*

Walking across the hardwood floors over to the entertainment center, Maymi turned on some music and it filled the room instantly relaxing some of the stress from her body. As she spun around and was headed back towards the appetizers' table the intercom buzzed.

Maymi hurried over to the box on the wall and pressed it. "Yes," she answered.

"Hey, let me up," Jensen said. "I want to see you."

"Do you know how early you and Casper are?" she asked. "The party doesn't start for another forty minutes."

"I know I am. I came early, so we could spend some alone time together before I get thrown to your girlfriends for an interrogation. Buzz me up, baby."

"Where's Casper?" Maymi asked, stalling for time.

"He's still at home getting ready. We ran into a problem at work, so he volunteered to stay and fix it. Aren't you going to buzz me up? Don't tell me you're scared to be alone with me in your apartment."

"Of course not," Maymi answered a little too quickly. "You were here before to pick me up for our first date."

"I believe that doesn't count since I was inside for less than five minutes," he tossed back. "You're beginning to make me think you won't be able to handle me until everyone else shows up."

"You're so wrong. Come on up." Maymi hit the button to let Jensen upstairs to her apartment.

Rushing over to the mirror, she checked her appearance one last time. She thought she looked good in the dark boot cut jeans and dark short sleeved shirt. Everything she was wearing tonight was cute and casual for the party, but still sexy enough to keep Jensen's eyes on her. She liked how his eyes got a shade darker when they lingered on her breasts. He thought she didn't notice, but she had more than once.

Maymi's fingers smoothed down a piece of her hair as a knock came on her door. She took one final look at herself before going over to it and opening it.

"Hey gorgeous," Jensen said, bending down brushing his lips across hers.

"Hi yourself," she answered. "You look very handsome." Maymi loved how he paired a button down white shirt with a pair of jeans and cowboy boots. He was sporting the casual look she told everyone to wear tonight.

"Thank you. These are for you." He pulled a bouquet of beautiful wildflowers from behind his back and gave them to her.

"Wow, they are stunning. Come on it so I can put these in some water." She took a step back from Jensen allowing him to move past her with a bottle of wine in his hand.

Closing the door, she took another whiff of the flowers surprised Jensen had given them to her again. He was steadily moving up in her book. She better keep a close eye on him since she loved fresh flowers. They were one of her favorite things, but she seldom got them from anymore, not since dating Hudson.

"Your apartment looks amazing. I can't believe everything you've gotten done," Jensen said, turning around to look at her.

"Truthfully, I started on some of it yesterday after work," she said going into the kitchen.

Reaching underneath the sink, she grabbed a vase then filled it with water. Maymi arranged the flowers before placing them on the table. "I've gotten flowers twice from you now. I believe I need to do something special for you next time."

Jensen set the bottle of wine on the table then gave her a smile that sent her pulsing racing. "You don't need to do anything for me. I only wished for you to give me a second chance and you did it."

"Why is spending time with me so important?" Maymi asked. She moved away from the table, grabbed a cork screw out of the drawer, then two glasses from the cabinet before facing him again.

"Here let me." Jensen took the items from her. He poured them two glasses of wine then handed her one.

"I guess it came from a mixture of curiosity and some hidden jealousy."

Maymi frowned. "I don't understand." She leaned against the counter and took a sip of the wine.

"I was curious about why you weren't intimidated by me. Most people don't stand up to me the way you had at Sinful. I was intrigued despite the fact; I wasn't going to admit it. I was attracted to the sexy woman I just got into an argument with."

"You do know that when I rented the property next door to your gym, I didn't know anything about you. All, I wanted was a placed to showcase my talents for baking," Maymi said, staring at him.

"I know that now, but back then weeks ago I wasn't thinking clearly. I thought you were purposely trying to get on my nerves with your bakery. I thought, what intelligent person would do something as crazy as you had done," he replied with a trace of humor in his voice. He was teasing her affectionately, but not maliciously.

"Okay, I understand that part, but why were you jealous?" Maymi asked. "I have nothing for you to be jealous of at all."

"I wasn't jealous of you actually, but the way you acted with everyone else including my brother but not me. You acted like just the sight of me found ways to piss you off."

Jensen drank his wine and studied her from his side of the counter. The soft sound of the music made it feel like they were on another date instead of waiting for more guests to show up at any minute. He was drawing her into him with his deep, penetrating eyes.

Placing his glass down, he walked towards her in a slow, predatory way that was all him. "Do you know how hard it is for me to stand over there and not touch or kiss you?" he asked, blocking her body between the counter and his big hard body.

Leaning closer, Jensen brushed his nose against her as he stared into her eyes without blinking. His mouth slowly lowered down to hers until his lips were only a breath away from hers before the loud, intrusive sound of the buzzer jerked them apart.

"Fuck! I hate that damn thing," Jensen snapped, stepping back from her.

Maymi glanced up at him and then over at the intercom. "I guess you were saved by the bell. You can try to get that kiss later," she challenged then walked away before Jensen could grab her.

Chapter Twenty-Seven

"I almost feel invisible from the way your eyes have been following Maymi around the room since I walked through the door. The two of you must have been doing something pretty good before I rang the buzzer," Casper teased him. "I know what I would have been doing with a hottie like Maymi."

Jensen stopped wondering what Maymi and her friends were huddled up in the corner talking about and gave his brother his full attention. Casper needed to learn when to talk and when to keep his big mouth shut.

"I told you not five minutes ago, it wasn't any of your business so why can't you just leave it alone?" He was no longer thinking about his missed kiss with Maymi, but instead he was worried what her friends might be putting into her head.

They had arrived about two minutes after Casper and the second they saw him they had dragged her away and Maymi hadn't been back over here since. He tried speaking to them, but Jazmaine and Tatum had ignored him completely. He got the real impression that they weren't totally on board with him being here.

He shouldn't care but a huge part of him did. They were really close to Maymi, a lot more than he was at this very moment. What if they thought of something convincing to make her not go through with the second date he had planned?

"Jensen, how about you tell me more about your date and don't tell me again you had a nice time. Remember, I know most of the women you have dated. Last night was the first time you ever called me up after one and wanted to talk about it. Something about Maymi stunned you, didn't it?" his brother inquired.

"Yes," he reluctantly admitted.

"Yes? That's it?" Casper complained, hitting him on the side of his arm. "You aren't going to tell me more? Come on. I think I had a part in you asking her out in the first place."

Jensen took one final look across the room and then faced his brother. "What makes you say that?" he inquired.

"You got jealous I had formed a bond so fast with Maymi and wanted to put an end to it, so nothing would happen between me and the woman you've wanted from first sight. Don't you dare deny it."

"I wasn't going to deny anything," Jensen confessed. Casper was completely right by calling it as he saw it.

He still had so many questions to ask Maymi about her life, but he didn't want to push her too much and end up scaring her away.

She presented a very tough exterior, but he still sensed something a tiny bit fragile about her that she might get hurt if he pressed her too hard. He saw a same glimpse of it the night she helped him after the attack, but he had only gotten a peek for a second then it was gone. Nevertheless, the sad look in her eyes had been way too old for someone so young; it came from something more than her mother's suicide.

The rare times she had flirted and even given him a smile were very appealing because her beautiful face had lit up. He liked the tranquil feeling that came with it making him want it again and again. The more he was around Maymi, the more special she was becoming to him.

The brightness of her personality was becoming something that he could start getting used to, if he allowed himself to go down that side road of his mind that he usually kept closed off.

"Aren't you going to tell me anything else?" Casper demanded, regaining his attention.

"No, I'm not, so leave it alone. Will you?"

"All I want—"

"Casper, I'm warning you," Jensen said in a low voice as Maymi glanced over her shoulder and looked in their direction. He waved at her, but she didn't wave back; instead, she turned around.

What in the hell was going on over there with her?

He was dying to know, but he wouldn't go over there. It wasn't his conversation to get involved it, but he knew for sure now that whatever Tatum and Jazmaine were telling Maymi concerned him.

"How could you invite him here for our party?" Jazmaine asked, staring towards the other side of the room.

"Are you talking about Jensen or Casper?" Maymi questioned as she took a quick glance over her shoulder and turned back around.

"Yes," Jazmaine and Tatum answered at the same time.

"I can't believe you have a problem with Jensen being here. It has to be him because neither one of you know anything about his brother. I thought you wanted me to go out with him to get to know him better."

Both women looked as if they were weighing her question before saying another word to her. She began to wonder if there was something they might be hiding that she should know about.

"Well," Tatum hedged.

If she had expected an easy yes or no from either one of them; she had underestimated her two best friends. They were always quick to give her advice and just as fast to back out when they didn't like the outcome.

"God, I'll ask her," Jazmaine said.

"We were wondering do you think you might be moving *too* fast with Jensen. You've only been on one date with him. Now you've invited him to our party. What has changed since we talked to each other?"

Maymi understood her girlfriends' concern, but they were reading way too much into her inviting him here tonight. She wasn't planning anything more than seeing how well he blended in with her friends.

Weren't they the ones who told her to start dating more instead of being chained to the oven at Sinful twenty-four seven?

Why wouldn't she start with the gorgeous guy not twenty feet from her business? Tatum and Jazmaine were sending her mixed signals about this. Why couldn't they just let her do as they warned her to do which was get back out there in the dating field?

"Girls, don't worry, I'm not planning on falling in love with him or anything; but I can't lie. He's a lot more fun to date than I gave him credit for. We might have gotten started out on the wrong foot, but he apologized and we are trying to see where things can go with us."

"I knew it," Tatum jumped in. "You're trying to become something more with him. I'm going to give you the same piece of advice my mother gave me when I was young. When a guy shows you who he truly is, believe him. I don't want you to get hurt. You usually don't move this fast with a guy."

She loved that her friends cared so much about her, but she wasn't getting blindsided by Jensen. She knew actually what she was doing. He was just a hot distraction for the moment, so she wouldn't spend hours and hours at work without anything else to look forward to outside Sinful.

"Guys, I swear to you that I see what is right in front of my face. Jensen isn't pulling anything over on me. We are only having fun with each other. Are you telling me that you don't want me to have an outside interest anymore?

"You two were the ones who told me to jump his bones the first time you laid eyes on him." She looked at Tatum and then over at Jazmaine who avoided giving her eye contact. She might not have been out on a date in a while, but she still knew the politics of the dance.

"You're right. We did, but you never listen to any of our advice half the time. Why did you do it now?" Jazmaine questioned. "Does it have to do with Jensen being so damn attractive?"

Maymi wasn't about to lose her mind over a handsome face and a killer body. Yet, something about the way Jensen treated her on their date was different. Almost like he could sense she was trying to be overly cautious, but he didn't allow her to do it. He actually looked at her while listening to the words coming out of her mouth; it was a nice change from the way her life had been going.

So, concern about Jensen hurting her early in their 'relationship' was nonsense and a waste of her time, not to mention theirs. For her life used to be about being adventurous and living in the moment. She wasn't going to let one bad first encounter keep her from having a good time with Jensen for as long as the winding ride lasted.

She shrugged. "I guess I was tired of pretending that I wasn't lonely, because I was. There were only so many pies and cookies I could bake before I needed something more fulfilling."

"Oh, I bet Jensen can give you something very satisfying," Tatum whispered. She glanced away from her over to Jensen who was staring at them from across the room.

"Stop it," Maymi hissed, hitting her best friend on the arm.

"You are making him uncomfortable. I don't want either one of you scaring him away. I'm actually having more fun with Jensen than I thought I would."

Spinning around, Tatum looked at her with concern. "Maymi, you know I love you. I just don't want you to get hurt," she said.

"I won't. I'm going into this with my eyes wide open, but I love the both of you for being so concerned about me. Now, how about make our visitors feel more welcome?"

Tatum touched her on the arm. "Maymi, we didn't mean to upset you talking about Jensen. We were only looking out for your well being. We love you and don't want to regret anything by jumping into a new relationship."

"I promise you that I'm not ever going to give Jensen enough power to do anything to me," Maymi insisted.

"Alright, we believe you," Jazmaine said, interrupting the conversation. "How about Tatum and I plate up the last of the food I saw in the kitchen. You go over there and talk to Jensen. I have to admit, he hasn't taken his eyes off of you all night."

"Jazmaine is right. He's been looking at you for a while," Tatum agreed. "I have to admit good looks must run in that family because Casper is gorgeous."

"You do like Casper?" Maymi asked, surprised. "Jensen's brother wasn't the type of guy you ever noticed before. I mean I told Jensen to bring him hoping he might catch your eye, but I'm shocked he did."

Tatum shrugged. "I don't know if I like him, but I can recognize that he's extremely *hot*."

"God, let me get out of here before I hear anything else from the two of you," Maymi said then spun around walking away from her friends. She had invited Jensen to the party and she hadn't spent more than ten minutes talking to him which was going to change.

Chapter Twenty-Eight

"I'm glad your friends finally came around with me being here tonight," Jensen said as Maymi closed the door behind Tatum and Jazmaine. "I thought for a minute I might have to leave because of the looks they were giving me."

Turning around, Maymi pressed her back against the front door. "Did they scare you?" she teased. "I mean apart, they can be tough, but together, they are a force like no other."

"No, I wasn't scared of them," he said, taking a step towards her. "Yet, I have to confess. I was worried what they might be filling your head with earlier about me. I mean did they make you think I was the Big Bad Wolf working his evil ways on you."

"Jensen, you should know something about me. I make my own decisions. I might ask for their advice, but in the end the choice is always mine. I've chosen to see where things are going between us but I'm doing it with my eyes wide open."

Moving a few more inches, Jensen placed his hand above her head on the door. He pressed his body against her as he stared into her eyes. "I'm glad you're a woman who knows how to make her own decisions. So does that mean I passed your test?"

"What test?"

"You know what I'm talking about. You invited me for one specific reason. It was to see how well I could handle being around your girlfriends. I think I passed with flying colors."

"You did better than I thought you would," Maymi admitted, placing her hand on his chest and giving him a shove away from her. "Casper even got to add another admirer to his little black book."

"I know," Jensen answered, pulling her back to him.

"What?"

"Casper was looking at Tatum. He even mentioned that he thought she was pretty good-looking. I hope he knows what he's doing with her. I doubt she'll put up with his constant flirting with other women."

"How about we keep the focus on us and not them?" she suggested, moving around his body.

"I like anytime I get to focus on you. I think it's way past time that we discuss what is brewing between us. I don't know how much longer I can fight it. Every time I get around you this invisible pull gets stronger and stronger."

"I'm not sure if I'm exactly following you."

"Maymi, you get what I'm telling you. Both of us have been fighting this since I stormed into Sinful," Jensen said, taking a step towards her.

"I don't know what in the world you are talking about," she lied. Maymi stepped away putting some useless distance between them. "I haven't felt any kind of pull; it's all in your head."

Jensen wondered how long Maymi was going to keep putting up this façade. "I never thought of you as a liar. We both know that you wanted to rip my clothes off the first time you saw me, and it has only gotten worse since our date."

He saw the hidden desire flare up in Maymi's soft brown eyes. She was slowly changing him for the better. He didn't stress about work as he used to before meeting her. He spent most of his time with her on his mind.

Was she thinking about him as much as he thought about her? He never worried about her when they weren't together, but Maymi brought out that side of him...

"So what if we have this burning attraction to each other," Maymi asked. "People have it all of the time with each other but never act on it."

Jensen paused in front of Maymi noticing how her breath caught in her throat the closer he got to her body. He wasn't sure if it was out of nervousness or fear, but either way he was going to put her at ease. He brushed the back of his finger against her cheek loving the smoothness of her skin.

"Honey, I'm not going to hurt you, but I want...need to make love to you. If you aren't ready, I can wait until you are ready to trust me more. I don't want to rush you into anything you might regret later."

"You aren't rushing me," she said, holding his eyes with hers. "I want to make love to you, too."

His cock grew hard against the front of his jeans at the idea of being inside of Maymi's wet, tight pussy. It had been months since a woman shared his bed and he was beyond ready to be with her.

He ran the pad of his index finger along her bottom lips. "I can't believe I didn't notice how stunning you were the first time I laid eyes on you; however, I promise to cherish every inch of your body before the night is over. I'll be gentle so it will be a night for both of us to remember. Baby, where is your bedroom?" Jensen asked her.

"It's down the hallway and the first door on the left."

Sweeping Maymi up into his arms, Jensen spun on his heel carrying her down the hallway to his bedroom. He walked her over the threshold and over to the bed gently laying her down in the middle. He stood back up taking in how good Maymi looked. The dark caramel of her beautiful skin looked breathtaking against the white sheets.

It was a sight he wouldn't mind seeing again and again if he had anything to do about it. Tonight was turning into something special for him, not just a one night stand. He was beginning to feel the stirring of something for Maymi and he wasn't ready to let her go until he worked through whatever it was.

"This is your last chance to tell me to get the hell away from you. I don't know how much self-control I will have once I see you totally naked. A man can only take so much temptation before he loses it."

"Has anyone ever told you that you talk too much, Mr. Lowe?" Maymi asked, leaning back on her elbows making her thick, black hair swing behind her.

"Sorry, baby." Jensen apologized. "Let me see if I can make it up to you."

Reaching for Maymi's leg, he pulled her body towards the end of the bed; then he slowly unzipped her boot, removed it and then tossed it over to the side followed by the second one minutes later. He stopped to stare at her firecracker red nail polish. He loved when a woman painted her toenails. In his opinion, it was one of the sexiest things she could do to her body.

"Undo your pants, so I can pull them off of you," Jensen demanded in a low voice. He watched as Maymi quickly unbuttoned her jeans, then slid them over her womanly hips.

Grabbing the hem of her blue jeans, he gradually pulled them down her toned legs and off her curvy body. For a few seconds he stopped doing anything else and stared at her sexy black skimpy underwear with a black and white bow at the top.

They were made to drive any red-blooded man out of his mind. It was definitely working on him. If he had known this was under her clothing all evening, he would have found a way to get rid of everyone else sooner. He didn't care if they were at Maymi's house.

Over the years, he believed the thinner the woman—the more he wanted her. Yet, seeing all of Maymi's womanly assets tonight made him realize what a fool he had been by missing out on something so beautiful and real.

"Take off your top. I want to see your breasts."

Night after night, he had lain awake alone in this bed dreaming about how she would look lying here next to him. Now it was time to see if his dreams lived up to his hot fantasies.

Moving around on the mattress until she was kneeling in front of him, Maymi looked at him and then glanced away as her fingers reached for the first button on her shirt.

"Don't you dare look away from me," he reminded her. "I want to watch your eyes as you get undressed for me, so I can see every single emotion you're feeling."

Nodding her head, she slowly undid one button, and then another one until her matching black bra was revealed. He stared at her luscious breasts as they almost spilled out of the lacy garment with every breath she took. It was barely enough fabric to cover her plump breasts.

Moving closer to the bed, Jensen reached out and tugged at the front clasp of the bra with his fingers. He growled in the back of his throat as her breasts fell free. He cupped the beautiful brown treats in his hands brushing his thumbs over her swollen nipples.

"Oh," she moaned. "That feels so good. It's been such a long time since I've gotten touched like this."

Jensen watched as Maymi tossed her head back causing her hair to spill over her shoulders. Leaning over her, he brushed a kiss along her neck listening with masculine pride as a soft moan of ecstasy escaped from her full, firm lips.

He couldn't help but smile against her skin; it had been a long time since a woman made him feel this *good* before actually making love to her. He pulled the remaining clothes off her body until Maymi was only left in her enticing underwear.

"Baby, why has it been such a long time for you?" he asked against her ear.

"Work. I've been trying to build my business more," she answered, running her fingers through his hair as his hands skimmed down her back and cupped her perfect, full ass.

"Well, tonight is going to involve something more pleasurable than any kind of sweets you can think of."

Lowering her back down to the bed, Jensen kissed his way down her perfect neck, over her creamy shoulders until his mouth paused at her swollen nipples. He blew on the right one until Maymi's sweet body bucked underneath his.

He ran his tongue over the tip before drawing the delectable treat into his mouth. Jensen decided right at that moment, she tasted better than any sweets at her bakery. He continued sucking, and nibbling until she began brushing her underwear covered pussy against the hard bulge in his jeans.

"Jensen, stop. I can't take it. I *need* you."

After a few more teasing nibbles, he let go of Maymi's nipple and planted a kiss between her breasts. Sliding his hand between their bodies, he grabbed her underwear and tore them from her body.

Without giving her time to react, Jensen slipped two fingers inside of her wet pussy, pumping in and out. The only sounds filling his bedroom was the noise of Maymi's moans along with the wet sounds of his fingers as they made love to her. He lowered his head back down to the other breast and sucked it back into his mouth, rolling the nipple with his tongue before biting down gently.

Maymi thrashed against him as her hands pulled at the sheets underneath her body. He continued sucking her breasts as his fingers pumped in and out of her welcoming heat. If she felt this good around his fingers, he might lose his mind once she was wrapped around his dick.

"Jensen, I'm so close," she panted, staring at him. The feverish look in her dark, brown eyes made him kick it up another notch.

Using his free hand, he spread her legs even further apart so he could give it to her better than he already was. Jensen wanted Maymi coming apart in his arms and in her bed. Nothing else mattered but showing Maymi how much he wanted her tonight and every other night after this.

"Let go, sweetheart. Show me how good I'm making you feel," Jensen encouraged.

He continued pumping his fingers in a little deeper so they brushed over her clit and minutes later, Maymi broke as her orgasm ripped through her body. He had to taste her...it was eating at him to have her on his tongue.

Jensen removed his fingers and slid down her body covering her pussy with his mouth licking at her cream as it poured from her pussy. He'd never sampled anything *so*... Shit, he didn't even have the words to describe it, but all he knew was he was going to take all she had to offer him and then some more when the right time came.

He heard Maymi scream again as a second orgasm started taking over. He licked all of the juices from her pussy until her body slowly calmed down. He gave her one final, long lick then kissed his way up her body until his mouth was pressed against her ear.

"Are you ready for me now?" Jensen whispered in a low voice. "Because I have plans to keep you in this bed for the rest of the night and way into the morning since I'm not ready to let you go yet."

CHAPTER TWENTY-NINE

Maymi had a very clear understanding of exactly what Jensen meant and she wasn't about to tell him no...not tonight when her body needed him so badly. She hadn't made love in a while, so she was more than ready to be with Jensen on a more intimate level..

"Yes, I'm ready for anything you want to give me," she answered, staring up at Jensen who was still completely clothed. "I know it will be better than anything I've ever experience before."

Excitement rushed through Maymi's body until she finally focused and took in Jensen's appearance. *Why wasn't he as naked as she was?* He was so gorgeous which meant he shouldn't have any clothes on. She still couldn't believe she was here with him like this. She'd never expected this to happen when she invited him over here tonight for Jazmaine's party.

Just looking at him made her mouth water and her pussy ache because he was the most perfect man she had ever laid eyes one. She wanted to see more of Jensen and the sad thing was he knew it too but he was making her wait. She wasn't embarrassed by her need to see him naked. She wouldn't even consider it as begging, but getting what she wanted. He probably wanted her to beg to his body.

"How much longer are you going to keep those clothes on?" she asked, sitting up on the bed. Maymi eased closer to the edge and reached for the first button on his shirt, but he brushed her hand away.

"What," she asked.

"Baby, if you touch me. I won't make it. I'm already wired too tightly as it is. I can't have you taking my clothes off or I'll lose control. I'll let you do it at another time," he told her. "I promise you."

Stepping away from her, Jensen's long fingers worked on the buttons on his white shirt then slid the fabric off his shoulders tossing it to the side. Next, he pulled off his cowboys boots and pitched them away from the bed.

Maymi's heart skipped a beat before pounding a little faster in her chest when Jensen unsnapped his jeans and slowly slid down the zipper. He pushed the tight denim over his hips then past his hard, muscular thighs until he was totally naked.

She stared. She couldn't help it. No other man she had been with ever possessed a body likes Jensen's. Totally naked...he had it all. Every single thing a woman fantasized about her dream lover was standing right in front of her and all she had to do was reach out and touch him.

He was breathtaking. His broad chest didn't have an ounce of hair which only made his six-pack more noticeable to her eyes and without even thinking she reached out to touch him. However, Jensen grabbed her hand and her eyes shot up to his.

"Remember, look but don't touch...not until I tell you to," he warned her in a low voice.

"I'm dying to touch you," she murmured.

"In a minute," he promised.

Nodding, Maymi eased her hand away from his and went back to looking at his striking male physique. He was buff with his trim waist, hard thighs but none of those things is what she was dying to know on a deeper, more personal level.

Her gaze inched its way back towards the juncture of his legs and stopped staring at the huge gift there tempting her. His cock was a sight of beauty with its thickness and large mushroom head. Her body creamed at the thought of him being buried deep inside of her pussy.

"Maymi, I can't wait any longer," Jensen said, drawing her attention away from his erection back up to his bedroom eyes. "I've got to have you, sweetheart."

"Neither can I," she confessed. "I want you so much that it's crazy."

She watched as Jensen grabbed condoms from his pants on the floor, tossed them on the top of the night stand for later. God, she was so ready for this. Maymi caught her breath as Jensen focused his desire-filled eyes back on her.

Coming back over the bed, he stepped between her thighs using his knee to spread them even further before lowering his naked body on top of hers. Jensen growled in the back of his throat the second his bare chest brushed across her nipples.

"Damn, baby. You feel so *good* beneath me," Jensen whispered as he grabbed her wrists, gently pulling them above her head.

"Thank—"

The rest of her words were cut off when he captured her mouth in a hot kiss and slid his tongue between her lips to tangle with hers. The movement of his tongue had her wondering what else would feel this amazing inside of her.

This is so wrong, but why does it feel so right, Maymi thought as Jensen's mouth left hers kissing a scorching path over to her earlobe. He licked the side once before drawing it into his hot mouth.

"Please," she cried, tugging at her held wrists trying to get free.

"Please what, Brown eyes." he whispered, hotly in her ear. "Tell me...what you like, want, *need* from me."

Maymi wasn't used to telling a man what she wanted from him. He usually gave it to her because he knew, but Jensen was different. He wanted to hear the words come from her mouth. Well, she could do it. She was too far gone not to.

"I—"

"What's wrong? Why can't you tell me?" Jensen asked as his body moved.

His hand slipped between their sweaty bodies until his middle finger eased inside of her pussy teasing her clit with slow, confident circular strokes. She whimpered, but continued to grind her hips against his hand keeping up with his movements.

"I want you," she panted.

Jensen's eyes stared down into hers. "I've wanted you since I demanded you pack up Sinful and disappear and it hasn't stopped. Hell, I'm not sure if it ever will."

Despite the fact, she made a promise to herself she wouldn't give in no matter what he did to her. Maymi was too far gone to even care that she as allowing Jensen to get the upper hand with her tonight.

"Damn woman...finally," Jensen snapped lifting his body from hers. "I didn't think I would ever hear those words from you."

She cried out in protest at Jensen leaving her, until she noticed him ripping open a condom package and slipping the sheath down over his massive erection.

Moving quickly, he re-covered her waiting body with his. Using his knee, he spread her thighs even further apart and slid his cock into her, continuing until he completely filled her.

Grabbing her legs, Jensen wrapped them around his waist. Her eyes widened as he seemed to go even deeper almost touching her womb with the tip of his thick dick.

"Ooh, you feel so fucking tight," he growled in appreciation. "I've have never been this snug in a woman before...I can barely handle it."

His hands tightened around her waist as he slid out and then thrust right back inside of her causing a friction that made her toes curl.

She couldn't take it. Jensen was making her body feel like it was going to come apart. She tried pushing him away, but he grabbed her wrists in one hand and held them down to the mattress above her head. Using his free hand, he slapped it against her ass making her pussy tighten even more on his cock.

"Don't fight me," he warned as he eased out of her and pumped right back into her again. "Let me have complete control tonight. Know that I'm the one in charge of everything you are feeling."

Maymi closed her eyes loving how her body just seemed to sing from intense moments of pleasure and lust. Why was she trying to fight this...him? Jensen knew what he was doing and she was going to let him do it for long as he wanted.

"Take it," she said, surrendering to his words. "I won't fight you anymore."

※

Jensen's heart pounded away inside of his chest the second Maymi's will broke and she gave in to him. He felt it the moment she gave her body over to him, so he could cherish it for the rest of the night.

He lowered his head whispering against her swollen lips. "You won't regret this, sweetheart."

Her eyes suddenly flew open and the lust shimmering in them showed him how much she wanted him too. The sight of her need turned him on as he continued thrusting into her welcoming heat. Jensen couldn't get over how tight and inviting Maymi's pussy was;

it was unbelievably addictive to his senses.

Being her with her like this finally outdid any fantasy he dreamt about night after night or thought of while he pleasured himself in the shower. Tonight was such pleasure and pain built into one that he wasn't sure if his body would be able to handle his orgasms.

Removing her legs from around his waist, he placed them against the mattress. Sweat poured down his body dropping onto Maymi's beautiful glistening body.

"Oh God, Jensen," Maymi panted. She raised her hips meeting him thrust for thrust; seconds before her orgasm took her over and her screams of pleasure filled the room.

Hearing her release, Jensen grabbed her hips and plunged into her over and over at a faster pace until his orgasms crashed through the entire length of his body shoving him over the edge until he could do nothing but collapse on Maymi's soft body.

Chapter Thirty

Soft kisses woke Maymi from her light slumber while long fingers stroked the skin above her navel. Turning in Jensen's arms, she smiled at him. "What do you call yourself doing, Mr. Lowe?" she asked, running a finger down the center of his chest.

"I think I'm touching the gorgeous woman in bed with me," he answered then gave her a quick kiss.

"Oh, now you're full of compliments. I believe I've found a way to cure that sharp tongue of yours."

"Any man is suddenly very agreeable after good sex with the woman he is drawn to," Jensen said, pulling her against him. "How are you doing? I hope I wasn't too rough with you."

The concern in Jensen's voice touched Maymi. She couldn't believe he was thinking about her well-being right now. "No, everything was perfect." She sighed. "I don't know if you could tell last night, but it has been a while since I've been with a man."

He hadn't wanted to mention it, but he could tell it had been a while for her. "Yes, I noticed. I mean I'm glad you decided to break your hiatus with me, but what caused it? I mean you're stunning. I know I haven't been the first man to ask you out. Did you swear off sex or something?"

Maymi wasn't sure if she as ready to talk about Hudson so soon with Jensen. His death still haunted her most days because she never got the chance to tell him goodbye. Their last conversation had ended in an argument and hours later he was dead.

"I never swore off sex officially but, after his death I couldn't think about being with anyone again," she admitted.

"Are you talking about Hudson?" he asked, softly.

She raised her head off Jensen's chest and stared at him. "How did you know Hudson's name? I never told you about him. Have you been asking about me behind my back or something?"

"No, I haven't been asking about you," he told her, sitting up in the bed. "You mentioned his name the night we had dinner. I wanted to ask you more about him then but I didn't. Are you ready to talk about him now?"

Everything in her being wanted her to scream no, but she couldn't keep hiding behind Hudson's sudden death as a justification not to get involved with another man. He wouldn't want that for her. The thing she had loved most about him was his patience with her. He allowed her enough time to warm up to him. He let her figure out if he was the right man for her.

"I met Hudson as I was leaving a florist shop," she said. "I was coming out and he was going in. The second our eyes connected, I had felt this instant connection towards him, but I didn't act on it because I wasn't looking for a relationship at that time. So, I just smiled at him and walked away; however, before I made it to my car someone tapped me on my shoulder and when I turned around, it was Hudson. He handed me a slip of paper with his phone number and told me to call him. He didn't officially ask me out on a date, but gave me the option of taking things further."

Jensen heard the emotion in Maymi's voice when she spoke about Hudson. He could tell that she had loved him very much. "How long did the two of you date?" he asked, trying to get her to open up to him some more.

"We dated for about five years. I loved him so much. He was so supportive of my career that when I decided to drop out of medical school and attend pastry school he was right there at my side through it all, even when my father told me it would be the biggest mistake I've ever made in my life.

"His words had literally crushed me, but Hudson told me to live my life for me and not him. I was hurt until he spoke those words to me and I realized he was telling me the truth."

"Why wasn't your father supportive of your career change?" he asked,

"My father believed I wouldn't have enough longevity with being a sweets chef as he called it. He's a very successful plastic surgeon back in Atlanta, Georgia. He always wanted me and my siblings to follow in his footsteps especially after my mother's death."

Maymi talked about her father almost like he was someone else's parent instead of her own. He couldn't believe her father wasn't supportive of his daughter's dreams. So what, she decided not to become a doctor like him. He still should have given her his unconditional encouragement with whatever she wanted to do with her time and energy.

"Did your father approve of your relationship with Hudson?"

Easing back from him on the bed, Maymi stared at him with a tense expression. "No, he didn't approve of it. In fact, he hated it and told me several times I should break things off with Hudson."

"Why?"

"Hudson was my father's business partner, like his second-in-command when it came to doing surgeries. The day I met Hudson at the florist, he had just gotten hired by my father. I didn't know how they worked in the same space everyday with each other and got anything done.

"If Hudson hadn't been the most talented plastic surgeon in Atlanta, my dad would have fired him in the blink of an eye. However, he was getting too many patients and needed an extra pair of hands to take care of all of their needs. He wasn't about to lose money out of pride.

"My boyfriend was so amazing. Hudson never allowed working with my father to stand in the way of our relationship. We were making plans to get married the day of his accident."

Jensen noticed tears filling up Maymi's eyes as she moved away from him on the bed. He hadn't wanted to bring back bad memories. But he couldn't move on and have any kind of a future with her if he didn't know everything about her past including the good and bad.

"If you don't want to talk about him anymore, we can drop it," he said, reaching for her but she slid away from his touch and got out of the bed.

Grabbing a sheet off the bed, Maymi wrapped it around her body and walked over to her bedroom window. She started out into the darkness putting some distance between her and Jensen. He had brought so many memories to the surface tonight. She wasn't thinking about telling him about Hudson when she invited him over here

tonight, but here she was remembering him.
Could she really find another man in the world who was anything like him?

Chapter Thirty-One

Jensen tried not to be hurt at Maymi's sudden withdrawal after the night they had spent together, because he could sense the barely controlled pain that was coiled in her body. When she moved away from his touch, he felt an extraordinary void that he didn't want to experience again from her.

Getting out of the bed, he snatched his jeans off the floor and slid them on before slowly making his way over to Maymi standing at the window. He stood behind her, but made sure not to touch her. He couldn't recall the last time he truly desired to take someone else's pain away as much as he did Maymi's tonight.

"Sweetheart, how did Hudson die?" he asked, gently.

She pulled the sheet tighter around her body then brushed a tear away from her eye with the back of her hand. The sight of her tears made his heart clinch tighter.

"Hudson loved motorcycles. I mean, he had a passion for them. He owned about six of them and was looking into buying another one for his collection. He spent most of his Saturdays outside working on them while I was inside testing out new recipes.

"I didn't mind it, because I realized it was something he was into before I came into his life. The one he loved the most was his 1984 Harley Davidson FXST Softail. He would take it out any chance he got, but we were constantly arguing about him not wearing a helmet. I never understood how a brilliant surgeon could be so dense."

"Did he tell you why he wasn't fond of wearing one?"

"In his macho opinion, it wasn't something cool to do. I was tired of hearing that same excuse over and over. We got into a huge shouting match one day about it before he went out on his Harley. I told him that he was going to regret not listening to me. He came back with, maybe something would happen to prove me right," Maymi said, choking out the last of the words.

Not being able to take it anymore, Jensen wrapped his hands around her shoulders pulling her back against his chest. He'd tried not touching her, but it was too much for him to handle. He just had to do it.

"Baby, tell me what happened," he whispered against the back of her head.

"He had gotten about five blocks from our house when a car ran a red light and clipped the back tire on his motorcycle. The impact threw him from the bike and the car smashed into a tree a few feet away.

"Somehow, Hudson found the strength to get up and make his way over to the three teenagers inside the car. He got all of them out and pulled them to safety before the vehicle caught on fire, but a few minutes later he collapsed and died at the hospital an hour later," she said, holding back fresh tears.

"How did you find out about all of this?" Jensen asked, spinning Maymi around so he could look into her eyes.

"One of the teenagers in the car he saved felt guilty about the accident and told one of the officers the truth. While I was at the hospital waiting to hear news about Hudson he came there and told me.

"I should have never said anything to him. He had been riding for over fifteen years without one accident. The day I told him something bad would happen, it did. I got him killed and I'll never forgive myself." Maymi lowered her head as her tears continued falling down her cheeks.

At first, Jensen was too stunned by her confession to take it seriously and then he saw Maymi was seriously blaming herself for the accident. She had nothing to do with Hudson's death.

"Maymi, look at me. I'm going to tell you something and I want you to hear me loud and clear."

At the sound of his voice, she lifted her head and looked at him. He could see the devastation in her eyes and it pained him she had been holding on to this guilt for so long.

"Baby, what you told Hudson had nothing to do with his accident. You only told him the truth and unfortunately, he didn't listen to your warning. If he had been riding without a helmet for years, nothing you told him was going to stop his behavior."

"I don't know if I believe you." She showed her disbelief in the tone of her voice. "I think I put a jinx on him or something."

Brushing her tears away with the pads of his thumbs, Jensen touched Maymi's chin forcing her to continue staring at him. "You need to believe me because it's the truth. You told me more than once how much Hudson loved you. Would he have wanted you to spend all of this time holding onto this blame?"

"No, he wouldn't have," Maymi answered in a soft voice. "He would've told me to mourn him for a second then move on with my life. He wasn't big on allowing the past to determine the future."

"I think he had the right advice for you," Jensen said, sliding his hand underneath the sheet covering Maymi's body. "I want you to live in the moment with me."

"I want to do the same thing," she said, looking at him with a little less sadness in her eyes.

She touched the side of his face with her hand and then ran her finger across his bottom lip. "I'm really beginning to like you a lot. You're a better man than I first gave you credit for."

He grabbed her hand kissing the tips of her five fingers. "You know what I'm beginning to think? That you're something pretty special yourself," he confessed.

Gathering her into his arms, he held her snugly. His body leaped to life just from the mere touch of Maymi's body against his. However, now wasn't the time for them to make love. She needed him to comfort her in a different way.

"Come back to bed with me," Jensen said, removing his hands from her body. He grabbed her hand pulling her back towards the unmade bed.

"Jensen, I'm not in the mood to do anything," Maymi said, stopping him halfway there.

Turning, he looked down into her face seeing the perplexing emotions there on display. "I won't lie. I would love to make love to you, but I think you need something else more now. So, come with me," he said again, tugging her towards the bed.

He got on first and scooted over before tugging Maymi down on the bed until she lay down next to him. He wrapped his arm pulling her to his body until they were cuddling.

"Baby, all I want you to do is relax and go to sleep. You opened up a lot to me tonight about Hudson. I know it had to take a lot out of you."

Maymi placed her hand on top of his squeezing his fingers. "Thank you for listening. I really hadn't talked openly about Hudson with anyone," she told him.

Her confession wrapped around him like a warm blanket. He was entirely caught up in his own emotions tonight as he began to feel some tangible bond forming between them.

"Sweetheart, you're welcome," Jensen answered.

Yet, Maymi didn't answer him. Instead he heard the soft sounds of her breathing. Jensen brushed her hair off the side of her neck planting a kiss below her earlobe. As she slept in the bed with him, he thought about where the next step of their relationship was going. He was positive he was more ready to see where it would go between them than her.

Chapter Thirty-Two

Early the next morning, Maymi sat at the kitchen table watching Jensen as he fixed them some breakfast. He was only wearing a pair of low fitting jeans that made his ass look absolutely perfect in her eyes. The muscles in his back moved every time he reached for something on the counter.

"I've never had scrambled egg whites with spinach before for breakfast," she admitted. "I'm not too sure if I'm going to like it. I'm more of a traditional pancakes and bacon lover. You know, the classics."

Jensen stopped what he was doing and looked at her. The sight of his bare chest had her squirming around in the kitchen chair.

"I'm hoping you will be willing to give it a fair chance. It's very healthy for you packed with a lot of nutrition."

Maymi glanced down at her body covered in Jensen's white shirt from last night. "Are you saying my body needs some help? I've never gotten any complaints about it before," she said.

Turning down the burner, Jensen moved away from the stove and came over to her. He moved her legs apart and stepped between them.

"Baby, your body is sexy as hell," he praised, running his hands over her breasts stopping to play with her nipples.

"Oh," she moaned, softly leaning into him.

"Did I have a problem with your body last night and less than twenty minutes ago," he whispered against her lips.

"No," Maymi answered, staring at Jensen.

"Good, don't ever doubt how much I want you," he said, stepping back. "But, I like your company just as much. You make me more relaxed than I've been in a very long time with a woman."

Jensen winked at her then went back over to the stove and worked on finishing up their meal.

"Tell me more about your life. I don't know that much about you. What are your hobbies, interests? What gets you excited?"

"I told you one of them on our date," he answered, taking the food off the stove.

He divided it up on two plates next to him and then sprinkled a little low fat cheese before bringing them over to the table.

"I still get a lot of comfort from staring at the stars. I believe it comes from the memories it brings up of my father." Jensen placed one plate in front of her and then took one before sitting down.

"Were you always close to your father?" Maymi asked then took a bite of her food.

She couldn't believe how good it tasted on her tongue. Who knew spinach for breakfast could be this tasty?

"He was my best friend. Casper was closer to our mother and I loved her as well, but I could tell my father anything. He was my biggest supporter," Jensen said then took a bite of his food.

"It must have been nice. Do you not have one bad memory of him?"

He swallowed before answering her. "I can't say that I do. Whenever I asked him something he gave me his full attention no matter how dumb the question might have been."

"Do you think you were your father's favorite?"

"Not at all, he gave me and Casper the same amount of attention. My brother never felt left out of anything we did together. My family was the best when I was growing up. Both of my parents are gone now, but I still miss them each and every day.

"When did they die?"

"I was a freshman in high school when my mother died and my dad lived long enough to see me graduate from college. I'm so thankful I had both of them for so long."

For the next several minutes, Maymi and Jensen continued eating in silence as both of them got lost in their own personal thoughts of their pasts. Neither wanted to think about memories, but they kept rushing back into their minds.

Placing her fork down on the plate, Maymi pushed it away and studied Jensen for a few minutes. "Finish telling me about yourself," she said, watching him closely.

Last night, she had opened up the deepest part of her soul to him. How could she not want him to give her a sneak peek into his as well?

Raising his head, he watched her thoughtfully for a moment. His eyes searched her face like he was reaching into her thoughts to figure out what she wanted him to tell her. "What do you want to know?" he asked, wiping his mouth was a napkin. "I thought I had told you about me already."

"You did, but that stuff was about your family. I want to know something about you," she said, pointing her finger in his direction. "What is the sexiest thing you've ever done? Do you have a guilty pleasure? Are you planning to open up to me some more?"

"Are you sure that you want to hear my craziest?" he warned.

"Yes, I do," Maymi answered, her curiosity piqued even more. She bet it was something *good* with the way Jensen looked.

"After spending three years working as a personal trainer at several local gyms, I decided one day I wasn't living my dream anymore. So I quit and checked into opening up my own gym; however, I ran into one problem. I didn't have enough capital to make a down payment on the place I wanted so to make some quick cash I—" Jensen stopped talking and just looked at her.

"Don't stop there," Maymi said, leaning across the kitchen table. "Tell me the rest."

A gleam came into Jensen's dark brown eyes as he also leaned across the space towards her."

"I was a male stripper for several years."

She was too startled by his confession to say anything. All Maymi could do was stare at Jensen as thought after thought raced through her mind. One thing was for sure, he was an ever-changing mystery.

"Did you take it all off?"

He gave her a look of utter disbelief as he fell back against his chair. "Is that all you have to ask me?" Jensen asked. "Some of my past girlfriends got upset by the fact I took off my clothes for money and no, I didn't get completely naked."

"I always thought male strippers were pretty sexy. So, I can't be upset that I'm dating one."

Jensen stared, complete surprise on his face and then he smiled at her. "Maymi, you never cease to amaze me," he said, getting up from his seat.

He came around the table and stood directly in front of her. "Care to play hooky with me today," he asked, pulling her out of her seat. "We can spend the day doing anything that you wanted."

"I hadn't planned on opening Sinful today because I was going to work on the books. I need to see what item is selling and the ones that aren't. I need to have a quick sale to get rid of them."

"I'll make a deal with you. Spend a few hours with me and then I'll take you to Sinful this afternoon to get that work done."

Maymi already knew her answer before Jensen made his suggestion. "I can spend the rest of the morning with you, but I need to be back at work later this afternoon. I can't afford not to get this done."

"Baby, I can do it," Jensen said then kissed her. "How about we take a shower together before I leave?" His hands roamed up and down her back stopping to cup her ass in his hands. He rubbed his erection against the front of her.

Linking her arms around his neck, Maymi stared up into Jensen's eyes. "Do you really want to take a shower or make love? You know the latter will cut into our time together."

"I'm a gambling man, so why don't we take our chances and see what happens?" he suggested, swinging her up into his arms and carrying her from the room.

"Jensen, put me down," she laughed. "I can walk on my own."

"How about you let me carry you and if you're good I'll give you a private dance later?"

Maymi instantly stopped squirming in Jensen's arms. She had already seen him naked but the mere thought of his powerful body moving to music shut her right up. She wasn't foolish enough to miss out on that opportunity.

Chapter Thirty-Three

"Do you plan on hiding out in your office every time there's a staff meeting?" an amused voice asked from the opened doorway.

Jazmaine took a minute to get herself together before glancing at Mr. Mashiro. She hoped he wouldn't search her out today, but he did it. She should have known knew better to think he wouldn't.

Turning her head, her eyes instantly connected with his across the room. He looked at her as if he were photographing her with his eyes for later. Maybe it was just the artist in him and she was reading *too* much into the situation.

"Mr. Mashiro, I wasn't hiding out as you called it," she corrected. "I was working on a project."

"How much longer are you going to keep telling me the same story?" he asked, coming into her office closing the door behind him.

She looked at the door and then back at Akito. "Is there a reason you closed my door?"

"Yes...privacy."

"Mr. Mashiro, anything we discuss should be done with an opened door so everything will be professional."

"Akito," he corrected. "This is the last time I'll tell you my name isn't Mr. Mashiro," he told her.

"I've heard other women here call you by your last name. Why is it different for me?" she questioned, watching him.

Sauntering across the room, Akito stopped at the corner of her desk. He placed one hand on the desk and the left one on the arm of her chair. "I don't have any interest in them but I want you to know you outside the workplace."

"Mr—" Jazmaine started and then stopped when his dark eyes narrowed at her. "Akito," she said and he smiled bringing an immediate softening to his handsome features.

"Don't tell me no," Akito said, "You're making me think the word yes isn't even in your vocabulary."

"I know the word yes," she answered.

"Great, I'll pick you up at six o'clock tonight at your place," he said, moving away from her personal space.

Jazmaine stared at him dumbfounded until it set in that she had been tricked by him into agreeing to a date. "No, wait. I wasn't agreeing to a date with you." She got up from her chair and hurried behind Akito.

Suddenly, he stopped and spun around causing her body to run into his. His hands wrapped around her upper arms holding her against his hard, tight body. "Today is the day I've spent weeks waiting for. I finally get to take you out on a date," Akito said with his sexy British accent.

The feel of his touch on her body was blocking all other thoughts from Jazmaine's head. Each time she saw him, the pull was stronger. She had to admit his appeal was devastating.

"Alright, I'll still keep my word and go out on this date, but I want to keep it simple, nothing over the top or expensive. I'm not into anything too flashy," she said, stepping back from him.

Looking down at her, Akito slid his hands into the front pockets of his perfectly tailored slacks drawing her attention to his hard muscular thighs.

"So, are you telling me I can't pick you up in a limo and take you to the best restaurant in town? I wanted to impress you, but all of your demands are tying my hands," he complained.

Yes!

Jazmaine swallowed down her smile. Her request had taken some of the wind out of Akito's sails. She liked that she gave him something to think about. He wouldn't be able to just take her on a cookie cutter date to gain points with her like he probably had done with numerous female groupies.

This time he would have to put more thought into planning a cute, simple first date. It would have to be something more towards her tastes instead of showing off how well he could toss his money around to bragging about who he was.

Chapter Thirty-Four

Jensen squeezed Maymi's hand as they walked around the park together. He couldn't recall the last time he simply went for a walk with a woman. Usually when he came to this certain park, it was to run or work out with Chloe when they were dating.

Doing this with Maymi was very relaxing with the sun shining down on their bodies. It was a feeling he could get used to experiencing again with the pretty woman next to him. He hadn't planned on falling for Maymi, but he was slowly becoming more and more interested in her to the point that he didn't want them seeing other people. He wanted them to be exclusive.

It wasn't like he had anyone else in his life at the moment, but he wasn't so sure about her. Yes, it might have been a while since she made love but she still could have an admirer lurking somewhere in the background. She was a beautiful woman on the inside as well as the outside, even Casper had noticed that about her.

"What are you thinking about so hard?" Maymi asked, bumping her shoulder against his arm.

Looking down at her, he saw the happiness in her eyes and didn't want to ruin it by pushing her too fast. She might not be ready to be in steady relationship with him. They might be going out causally, but he wanted to be more than just her dating buddy.

He pulled Maymi off the trail over to a park bench away from the other couples walking around. Sitting down next to her, he let go of her hand and placed his hand on her thigh. She glanced at it and then back up at his face.

"Is there something wrong?" she questioned.

"Yes and no," he answered, honestly.

"I'm not following you," Maymi said.

"Sweetheart, I've really been enjoying the time we have been spending together lately. I know we've only been on a few dates, but those have made an impact more than any others I've done before."

"I've had a good time too, Jensen. We've had a lot of enjoyable times together with everything being so comfortable and neither one of us putting pressure on the other one."

Jensen hesitated, torn by conflicting emotions after hearing Maymi's words but he went ahead with his plan. He wanted Maymi as his girlfriend— *his woman.*

He couldn't see her out on a date with any other man but him. She wasn't the package he thought he would fall for, but she was everything the universe knew he needed.

"I feel the same way and that's why I want us to officially become a couple," he said.

Maymi's eyes widened in alarm then she slid away from him on the bench putting some distance between them. He understood her fear at getting involved with him because of the love she had shared with Hudson, but he was dead and he wasn't. He was right here in front of her ready to take things to the next level.

"Don't you think we should keep things as we have them? I mean, what's wrong with us going out and maybe making love afterwards. We don't need to put a title on anything."

Was she actually suggesting friends with benefits?

Stretching his arm across the back of the bench, Jensen moved back towards Maymi pleased when she didn't move back from him. He moved his other hand up and down her leg trying to relax some of the tension from her body.

Maymi agreeing to do this was a lot bigger step for her than him. The last man she was involved with died tragically, but Maymi had to understand that their relationship would be totally on a different level.

"I disagree with you. There's a lot wrong with us trying to be friends with benefits. I want to introduce you as my girlfriend to as many people as I can. I want to show you off and be proud you're mine and no one else."

She reached out and touched his hand. "I can't guarantee if I can completely be in a committed relationship with you a hundred percent."

"Maymi, no one can guarantee anyone a hundred percent of anything because life doesn't work that away. All I'm asking is we give it a chance and agree to be exclusive. I don't want you to feel pressured, but I do want you to be solely mine."

"Jensen, I wasn't expecting you to toss all of this into my lap out of the blue," Maymi said, looking at him with confusion. "I need some time to wrap my head around all of this. I thought we were only taking each day as it came since we're both so busy with our jobs."

Maymi quickly stood up causing him to jump up right after her. *Had he spoken too soon and scared her?* Jensen saw he might have spoken too soon. He hadn't meant to tell her any of this today, but everything just came out before he could stop the words.

"Babe, let me take it back a few steps. I think I gave too much at once." He took a step towards Maymi causing her to move back even further.

"No, give me a few days to think about this. I need to figure out what is going on with me. You seem to have figured it out for yourself already."

"I haven't figured out anything yet," Jensen correct, wanting to ease her worries. "All I do know is the time we have spent together was pretty damn fantastic. What man wouldn't think about furthering those moments?"

Maymi walked back up to him and placed her hand on his chest. She stared up into his eyes and he got lost in their dark depths.

"Give me two days and I'll have an answer for you. Am I asking too much?"

Jensen wrapped his arm around Maymi's waist holding her against him. She was right. He had thrown her a curve ball by demanding a commitment from her. He wouldn't have appreciated if she had done the same thing to him, tossing out demands he wasn't ready for.

"Alright, I'll give you two days to get your head together, but I'm going to warn you that I'm going to expect an answer."

Standing on her tiptoes, Maymi planted a kiss on his lips but moved back when he tried to deepen it. "Don't worry, I'll have an answer for you," she whispered then stepped back from him. "Let's go and finish our walk before you need to take me to Sinful."

He grabbed her hand again giving it a light squeeze. She might have been surprised by his confession, but at least she hadn't shot down the idea. Jensen decided to be patient enough to wait the two days, but if she took longer then he was going to seduce her into seeing things his way—the right way.

Chapter Thirty-Five

The following night Jensen sat on the couch at his house trying to ignore the look Casper was giving him. It was one of complete disbelief like he couldn't believe the words that just had come out of his mouth. He didn't see what the problem was.

"You can't be my brother. What did you do with him and how can I get him back?" Casper complained.

Sighing, he mentally kicked himself for even telling his brother about his conversation with Maymi while the basketball game was on. He had made the mistake of thinking he could confide in his brother about something so important to him.

He glanced to his right and found Casper still watching him. "I'm giving her a chance to get her emotions together. She came out of a long, very loving relationship with a man who died on her suddenly. I can't force her into doing anything she's not prepared for. I don't want to lose her. She might be the one and I have to give this thing between us a real chance."

"Are you falling for her?" his brother asked, surprised. "I thought you were..."

"I was only what..." Jensen demanded in a low voice.

"Only having a good time with Maymi. It never crossed my mind you might want something deeper with her. You never have done deeper before not even with Chloe who seemed like your perfect fit. Maymi is so different from her. I just don't see the two of you being an official couple."

"Why not?" he questioned, watching his brother closely. "Do you think we wouldn't be good together or something?"

Jensen wanted to know what Casper was thinking. Maybe it was the same fears Maymi was harboring and that's the sole reason she asked him for time to think about them.

"I shouldn't have said anything," his brother said then glanced away from him back at the television.

"Don't you dare hint at something like that and then not go through with it. I need to know what is on it that head of yours."

Casper glanced away from the television and back over to him. "Maymi isn't the standard you always seem to fall for. Your past female companions may have been stunning to look at, but they didn't have much going on upstairs."

He was instantly insulted. He hadn't been only dating airheads these past few years. "Chloe wasn't an airhead," Jensen pointed out.

"No, she's a world class bitch. I swear I've never met a woman as nasty as her. I still don't know how you dated her for so long. Did she give you instructions how to have sex in the bedroom? She comes off as a super control freak."

"Hell no! Besides, we looked good together and that was what I was going for back then." Jensen couldn't deny the fact they had always turned heads when the two of them entered a room. However, he had grown since that time and he wasn't attracted to those women anymore.

Why couldn't Casper understand or believe he had changed?

"See and there lies the problem. Maymi looks nothing like Chloe. She's beautiful with sexy curves in all of the right places. I mean I did a double taken when I first saw her. She's not on the same level as Chloe. How can you be serious about Maymi? For as long as I've know you, you have dated women a size four or smaller."

He *never* thought Maymi might not want to date him because of her weight. He didn't find a thing wrong with her at all. She was perfect in every single way that counted. If he had needed Chloe or another copy of her, he wouldn't have ever pursued Maymi. He wanted to be with her and no one else.

She was stunning, clever, hilarious and had a body that made him want her all day and night. Comparing her to another woman hadn't crossed his mind once, why would it?

"Do you think that could be the actual reason she isn't ready to give me a definite answer?"

His brother shrugged. "I can't read her mind, so I can't be sure of her reasons. All I know is she doesn't come across like the type to rush into anything without thinking it through."

Jensen couldn't deny Maymi probably wouldn't tell him her answer until she was good and ready, but he hoped it would be the one he wanted to hear.

~~

Across town, Maymi walked around her apartment still thinking about what Jensen had proposed to her. Was she ready to let Sinful come second in her life to romance? The love she'd shared with Hudson was so special. His support of her had been constant and never changed when he got into fights at work with her father over it. He seldom allowed anything to come between them.

Jensen, on the other hand, was totally the complete opposite of Hudson. He had wanted her gone from his neighborhood from the very first second the sign went up at her bakery. They had got into heated fights about it on more than one occasion. Nevertheless, they had come together under the most oddest of circumstances.

Her problems involved why she was even giving his suggestion any thought of them becoming an official couple. Could it come from Jensen literally being the perfect image of tall, dark and handsome?

She couldn't afford to make a mistake with her decision and allow him to take her concentration off of Sinful if it wasn't necessary. Sure, everything was going outstandingly for her, but that came from all the work she was putting into her decisions about business each and every day.

Jensen came into her world when she wasn't expecting it, but what man that looked like a professional fitness model, wanted to devote his time to building a relationship with her? She created the things fitness professional like him warned his clients to stay away from. Could they really promote their passions without stepping on each other toes?

Her father told her when she was younger and when she was still listening to his every word, a man could tell her anything, so she should judge him by his actions. They always spoke the truth.

So far, Jensen had been back and forth with his actions. First, he was harsh and critical, but he changed showing a sweet much more romantic side to his personality. She felt like Jensen was showing her the man he really was.

Maymi stopped wandering around her apartment as something hit her. Subconsciously, she had been putting Jensen through tests and he had passed every single one she had gave him without knowing it.

Why aren't I with him right now instead of pacing around this big, lonely apartment?

She rushed over to her cell phone on the kitchen counter, picked it up and then dropped it back down. No, she wasn't going to call him tonight. Jensen needed to worry about her decision for a few more hours. She might be agreeing to this 'couples' idea of his, but she was still going to stay her own person.

If Jensen couldn't handle that part of her decision, he might have to give himself more time to get used to the idea. She had been independent for way too long to drop everything and blindly fall in line behind a man.

Humming to herself, Maymi spun around and headed towards her bathroom for a shower, and then she was going to play a game on her computer before going to bed. Tonight, she was going to take time for herself since everything was going so perfectly for her.

⁂

"Damn man, are you going to stand there all night staring at it?" Kenny snapped. "Toss it through the bitch's window and then we can get the hell out of here."

Turning, he glared at Marty standing to his left. "At least I stayed here and confronted her instead of running away like you did. I wasn't a coward."

"Listen, I wasn't a fucking coward. I just couldn't afford getting caught by the cops. I had to think about myself first. Didn't I come back here with you to get this done? So do it!" Marty shouted.

"The bakery chick shouldn't have gotten involved in our business with Jensen. Shit, I still can't stand that asshole," Kenny complained. "He had no right to throw us out of his gym."

"Well, we can get back at both of them by doing this. I saw them at the park today holding hands. I guess she's his girlfriend now. I wouldn't have ever given up Chloe for her."

"Marty, I don't give a fuck about Chloe or this bitch. All I want to do is teach her a lesson."

"Well, you're spending more time talking than taking actions against Maymi. Show her that she needs to keep her nose out of other people's business."

Kenny glanced back at his buddy, then down at the rock in his hand before he grinned and flung it through the huge bay window. The sound of glass shattering, ricocheted through the desert streets.

"Come on. Let's give her something else to think about before we leave," Marty said as he went through the window walking over the broken glass.

Kenny paused, looking around making sure no one was around before he bent down and picked up the can of black spray paint. Standing back up, he hurried through the opening behind Marty ready to leave his mark on Sinful.

Chapter Thirty-Six

The loud ringing of the phone woke Maymi from a deep sleep and after she wiped the sleep from her eyes, she reached for the phone.

"Hello," she whispered in a sleepy voice.

"Ms. Monroe," the man asked in a deep voice filled with authority.

"Speaking, can I help you with something?"

Maymi scooted up in the bed and narrowed her eyes trying to make out the time across the room on her dresser. She noticed it was a little after eleven o'clock. Who was calling her this late? She had to get up in about five hours for Sinful.

"I'm Officer Terrence. I'm calling to tell you about a vandalism at your bakery. Do you think you can come down here?

The words woke Maymi completely up. She reached across the nightstand and turned on the lamp by the bed. She tried desperately to stay calm, but her heart was racing.

"I must have misunderstood you. Did you tell me someone broke into my bakery?" she asked, hoping she had misheard him.

"There were two guys, but we caught them as they were coming back out through the broken front window," Officer Terrance told her. "Ms. Monroe, you really should get down here. I need you to see if you know these two men. Also, I think it might be best you call someone to be with you. The damage is pretty extensive."

With a shaky hand, she flung the sheets off her body and swung her feet down to the floor. "I'll be there in about fifteen minutes."

"I'll still be here taking picture as evidence," he informed her then hung up.

Jumping out of bed, Maymi stripped out of her pajamas and then grabbed some clothes, quickly tossing them on. She slipped on her shoes, grabbed her purse and car keys off the dresser and dashed out the door. She had to get to Sinful to check out the damage. Hopefully, it wasn't as bad as Officer Terrence described it to her over the phone.

⁂

No! No! No! Maymi's mind silently screamed as she pulled up in front of Sinful. She swallowed hard, trying not to let her misery and anger consume her. Stopping her car, she stared at the total destruction right in front of her eyes. Turning her life-long dream vision of Sinful inside of her head into this building had taken a long time, but now it was completely destroyed.

Getting out of her car on weak legs, she slowly made her way towards the shattered, broken bay window. The front of her bakery used to be picture perfect with the hot pink lettering across the glass.

Maymi was oblivious to the glass crunching underneath the bottom of her shoes as she walked into her former successful business. She took small steps around the once welcoming front area of Sinful.

She took in all of the broken cases and her grandmother's award winning desserts now smeared across the checkered floor. Nothing was as she had left it earlier in the day. She had only been here about six hours ago and everything was in its place.

Now, Sinful was a memory. This rubbish surrounding her never was what she wanted for her amazing grandmother. She worked so hard to give this place every special touch she could for her.

"Ms. Monroe."

Turning, she saw a tall, bald police officer standing behind. She remembered him. He was one of the police officers who came here after Jensen had gotten attacked. Maymi hurried and wiped away the tears from her eyes with the back of her hand.

"Yes," she said, walking up to him.

"I'm sorry about your business, but at least we caught the two guys. Do you have a few minutes to look at some mug shots?" he asked.

"I've time to do it." Maymi watched as he pulled two mug shots from a folder in his hand.

"Do you know these two men?"

She took the pictures from Officer Terrence and gave them a

long look before handing them back to him. The memories of their two faces were pure and clear. She wouldn't ever forget them.

"Yes, I know them. They were the same two men who attacked Jensen outside of Fitness 24."

"Are you talking about Mr. Jensen Lowe?" he asked, shoving the photographs back into the black folder.

"Yes," Maymi answered. "Did this vandalism have anything to do with Jensen's attack?"

"I believe it does, but they aren't admitting to anything. However, as soon as I get anything more I will contact you," Officer Terrence informed her. He turned on his heel and then spun back around. "Once again, I'm sorry about Sinful. Do you have anyone who can come and help you clean all of this up?"

Maymi already knew Jazmaine and Tatum would be upset with her if she didn't call them about this. Whether or not she was going to call Jensen was still something she was debating. She wasn't sure if she wanted him here.

"I can call my friends, but I don't see what good it would do. This place is totaled. Nothing can be saved. My bakery is ruined."

Officer Terrence gave her a sympathetic look before walking back across the glass on the floor and leaving her alone with all of the destruction.

Taking a deep, unsteady breath she tried holding back her tears but everything became too overwhelming. She couldn't handle this, not alone. Maymi reached into her jacket pocket, pulling out her cell phone. She dialed the number of the person she wanted to see the most.

~

Wrestling with the covers, Jensen pulled them off his naked body. He took a quick glance at the clock frowning when he noticed the time. Who in the hell was calling him at one o'clock in the morning? He knew it wasn't Casper, because he brother was asleep in the guest bedroom since he decided it was too late for him to drive back home after watching the basketball game.

"Hello," he said, answering the phone.

"Jensen, I need you," Maymi's soft voice cried.

He instantly jumped up in the bed, turning on the light. The pain in her voice terrified him "Baby, what's wrong?"

"It's...it's Sinful. They destroyed it. I can't come back from this. I've lost everything. I need you to come here, please."

He didn't understand what was going on. Maymi was telling him something, but he was lost. He had to get to her, so he could help her like she called him to do.

"Sweetheart, I'm not following you. Take a breath and tell me again what happened to you. Are you trying to tell me something happened at the bakery?" The phone went silent for a few minutes, but Jensen knew Maymi was still there because he could still hear her breathing in the background. "Honey, can you make me understand better?"

"They broke the window and then sprayed painted the entire front of the store. All of the cases are open and food is everywhere. I can't fix it."

Rushing out of the bed, he rushed over to his closet and yanked the first things he saw off the hangers. "Who do this? Did the cops catch the guys?" he asked, holding the cell phone against his shoulder while he pulled on his pants. "How did you find out about this?"

"I got a phone call about twenty minutes ago. The alarm got tripped and the cops called me. Please hurry up. I need you here with me," she said, choking on her words. "I'm going to call Jazmaine and Tatum after I hang up with you. They aren't going to believe this."

"Maymi, I'll be there in less than twenty minutes. I want to make sure you will still be at Sinful. I'm going to wake up Casper and bring him with me. Just take a breath and I'll be at your side." He hung up the phone and tossed it on the rumpled bed before he finished getting dressed. Maymi needed him and he wasn't going to waste anymore time getting to her.

CHAPTER THIRTY-SEVEN

"How is she doing?" Casper asked him. "I mean we have been working for hours getting this place cleaned up, but Maymi is walking around like she's in a trance."

Jensen laid a piece of wood against the wall staring at Maymi across the room. He was just as concerned as Casper about her. When he had first gotten here, the sight of Sinful shook him so badly that he wasn't able to say anything to her.

What hurt even more was the two assholes he had the fight with were the ones who did this.

"I think she's going through the motions, but she's in denial. She telling everyone Sinful is ruined, but I believe in the back of her mind she thinks she can get this bakery back up and running. We both know it will take a lot of money to make that happen and Maymi doesn't have it. She told me how much she had to do getting this far."

"Damn it. I wish I could've caught Kenny and Marty. I would have beaten them within an inch of their lives. They aren't going to get away with this. I like Maymi a lot. She's one of the sweetest people I have ever met."

"I love her," Jensen said, without thinking and then paused as the shock of discovery hit him full force. A new and unexpected warmth surged through his body at the thrill it gave him to speak the words.

Intense astonishment touched his brother's face as he stared at him. "Have you told Maymi this?"

"No, I just now realized it myself. I knew I was falling for her when we took the walk in the park, but I hadn't put it together yet. However, when she called me tonight crying and upset about the break-in at Sinful I couldn't get here to her fast enough. All I could think about was taking away her pain."

"Big brother, I think you have been bitten by the love bug. Who knew it could happen to you?"

Mixed feelings surged through Jensen. He knew without a doubt in his mind that he was in love with her. Somehow it had eased up taking over his heart, but he wasn't scared of it. In fact, he fought down the urge to rush across Sinful and tell Maymi. He couldn't tell her here, not with everything she had going on tonight.

Maymi hadn't even given him an answer about being an official couple. How would she take the news he was in love with her? She might be puzzled by his abrupt change in his mood. A strange and disquieting thought began to race through her mind. What if she didn't want anything more from him than what they had?

The thought tore at his heart and stabbed his insides. It was impossible for Jensen not to have a little fear at what was going on inside of Maymi's head. Shit! She could start blaming him for this and not want a thing to do with him. He wouldn't get the chance to make her see how good he could be for her. All of these ideas gnawed away at his confidence and a panic like he'd never known before welled in his throat.

"I never thought it could happen to me," Jensen said, jumping right back into the conversation, "but I'm concerned. Maymi might not want me. She has enough to deal with now. I'm sure declaring her love for me isn't one of them."

"Jensen, you shouldn't assume you know what Maymi is going to tell you. She might feel the same way. Weren't you the first person she called? Not her two best friends Jazmaine and Tatum, but you. That has to count for something."

Jensen looked back over at Maymi staring at her as she moved to the other side of the room. She touched some of the spray paint tags on the wall and brushed tears away from her eyes.

Turning his back to her, Jensen grabbed Casper by his arm. "Look at her. She's heartbroken and being with me caused some of it. Marty and Kenny came after the bakery because I kicked them out of Fitness 24. I can feel her pain all the way over here. She isn't going to ever look at me the same again."

"Look, we both know this place is gone. She won't ever be able to get it back into the same shape it once was. So, how about you think of a way to give her back her dream?"

Letting go of his brother's arm, Jensen folded his arms over his chest. "What are you talking about? How can I help Maymi? I would do anything to take all of this pain away from her."

"You have to give her something new to focus on instead of what she has lost," Casper suggested.

Standing there, Jensen tried to figure out how he could take his brother's suggestion and make it happen for his woman. All Maymi ever pushed for in her life was to have a bakery making all of her grandmother's famous recipes. She'd had it until a few hours ago when her world got turned upside down. He had to think of something to give that rush of feeling back to her. Seeing, Maymi with tears in his eyes was tearing at his heart but it wasn't like he had a vacant building just sitting around…wait a minute!

"Health Pro," Jensen said as he uncrossed his arms. "Casper, I have it!"

"I'm not following you," his brother said, frowning in his direction.

"I know how to get Maymi's mind off of all of this. I can buy this building from the property owner and combine it into Fitness 24."

"I don't think that will help Maymi," Casper said softly, staring at him with confusion. "She'll hate you forever."

"No, this happening to Sinful might be the best thing ever for me and Maymi. I can—"

"What in the fuck did you just say?" a female voice hissed.

Jensen spun around and his heart dropped to his feet when his eyes landed on the look of pain on Maymi's face. "Maymi, you misunderstood me." He took a step towards her, but Jazmaine jumped in his path followed by Tatum. Over their shoulders, he watched in sheer agony as Maymi turned away from him and ran towards the front door.

"Maymi, baby, please wait. It's not what you think. You misunderstood me," he yelled and then tried to go after her, but Tatum held her hand up stopping him.

"She didn't misunderstand one word out of your mouth," she snapped, pointing a finger in his face.

"I knew you weren't to be trusted," Jazmaine said, jumping in. "Stay the hell away from our best friend. Don't you dare show up at her place! Because I will be there, and to make sure you don't try anything, I had a date for later tonight, but I'm going to cancel it so I can be there for her."

He brushed Tatum's hand off his chest. "Neither one of you can keep Maymi from me. I will talk to her if I want to. She has to understand. I wasn't actually saying what happened to Sinful was a good thing for me."

"We all heard you loud and clear," Jazmaine said, turning away from him. "Now, I need to go and check on my best friend to make sure she's okay."

"Casper, I don't have a problem with you," Tatum said, looking past him over to his brother. "However, you should make sure your brother understands he isn't welcome around Maymi anymore." She glared at him, pivoted and then hurried behind Jazmaine out the door.

"The hell I will allow those two to tell me what to do," Jensen uttered. He started for the door, but was caught by the back of the arm.

"No, you can't follow them."

"Get the fuck off of me," he yelled, jerking his arm away from Casper.

If his brother thought now was the time for him to take Maymi's side, he was crazy! She was right outside thinking the worst possible thoughts and he had to fix it.

"Will you stop acting like a madman," Casper hollered. "You aren't going to get anywhere with Maymi tonight, so why chase after her."

"I'm going after her because I love her. She needs to know how I feel."

"She will but not tonight. Let's finish boarding up the windows, and you can finish telling me what you want to do with Health Pro. I think I know, but I want to hear it from you," Casper said.

Jensen thought about arguing, but deep down he hated that his brother was right. As much as he wanted to see Maymi, Jazmaine and Tatum weren't going to let him within touching distance of her tonight. Hell, it might take a few days but he wouldn't wait too long to get Maymi back.

"Fine, I'll listen to you this one time but I'm not going to allow too much time to past."

He wasn't going to let Maymi push him out of her life, if he had to camp out in front of her house, he would do it to talk to her. She wasn't going to get away from him before they cleared the air.

CHAPTER THIRTY-EIGHT

Three weeks later...

He couldn't wait any longer. He had gone to her apartment, but either Jazmaine or Tatum answered the door instead of Maymi. He hadn't laid eyes on her since that horrible night at Sinful. When he called her cell phone, it went straight to her voice mail and she never returned his calls. Jensen got the feeling that Maymi wasn't even listening to his messages anyway.

At least Marty and Randy had finally pleaded guilty to the charges against them instead of making Maymi attend a trial. He wouldn't have known any of this if he hadn't heard it on the local news. He doubted Maymi would've picked up the phone and given him a call.

"I knew Krissy was lying to me. You are up here. Why are you standing there staring out of the window?"

"Chloe, what are you doing here?" Jensen demanded, glaring at his ex-girlfriend. She wasn't the type of woman to go away without a fight.

He hadn't heard from her in weeks and he wasn't upset about it. He should have known she would have come to him. It was all over town about the incident at Sinful and how he bought the property at a cheap price.

"I don't know why you aren't happy to see me. I haven't done anything to you. I thought you would be happy to see a friendly face since Maymi hates the mere mention of your name."

"What Maymi feels for me isn't any of your business," he snapped. "I want to know why you think it is."

Chloe gave him a wide-eyed innocent look. "Will you stop yelling at me? I'll tell you again that I'm only here as a friend. I'm telling you the truth."

Moving away from the window, Jensen walked a little closer to her. "We aren't friends. You came here for another reason. Spill it."

"Maymi didn't deserve you. We understood each other, but instead of being mad at her for dumping you, you're standing there screaming at me. I don't get it at all. Shouldn't you be more excited?

"Sinful is no longer a threat to Fitness 24. There's no way she's coming back from this. All you have to do is sit back and wait for your gym to get even bigger. It has been a damn good several weeks for you."

Standing in the middle of his office, Jensen stared at Chloe wondering where in the hell she had gotten this idea of hers from. Why would she ever think he would be thrilled about his girlfriend losing her business? He loved her…No, wait he was in love with Maymi from the way she smiled at the smallest gifts he had given her down to the way she defended her friends with everything in her.

For weeks now, he had fought what was right in front of his face, but the truth hit him full force the night he was helping her at Sinful. He adored Maymi more than anything he could ever own. Nothing was more important than holding her in his arms.

Chloe was in front of him truly thrilled about Maymi's loss. She actually hunted him down at work thinking she still had a chance with him.

Jensen knew Chloe had a mean streak, but he never thought she would take her bruised ego this far. Maymi lost her dream, but he was working hard on getting it back for her. Gaining Maymi's trust again might be hard, but he was willing to do anything to do it, because he had found the woman he was meant to share his life with for the next fifty years or longer. He wasn't about to let Chloe snatch it all away from him with her hopes of them being a couple again.

"You're wrong," Jensen said. "I'm not excited about any of this. I didn't want Maymi to lose everything because of Kenny and Marty. You need to get over our breakup and let me go."

Chloe stared back at him with false innocence plastered on her face. "Jensen, I never said I was pleased about what happen to Little Miss Bakery. But, come on. Honestly, how long do you think the two of you could have lasted?

"I mean you're molded for fitness magazines and she's a chocolate chip cookie away from being in a Jenny Craig commercial. The two of you don't belong in the same room with each other. How could you be serious about wanting to date her?"

"I don't know what you're talking about," Jensen interjected as his patience started to wear thin.

"I mean a five should stay with a five and pretty people like us who are in the double digits should never date down. Jensen, I thought so much better of you. Didn't you learn anything from dating me?" Chloe demanded.

He was furious!

Jensen clenched his teeth trying desperately to swallow down some of his anger. He couldn't afford to lose his cool.

"Chloe, I'm not dating down. I don't know where you got that idea from, but it wasn't from me. Maymi isn't beneath me and I want you to understand how much I love Maymi. She isn't going anywhere. Sinful is a part of her like Fitness 24 is for me. We both get immense satisfaction from owning our own businesses. I won't allow you to talk down about her to me or anyone else. Don't ever let me hear you or you will regret it."

Her nostrils flared with fury. "How are you going to stop me?" She spat out the words contemptuously at him. "I mean...will Maymi really believe you cared about Sinful getting closed down. I know she can't even be that stupid."

"Chloe, get out before I throw you out of my office. I've warned you about talking about my girlfriend and I'm not going to warn you again."

Jensen was surprised by how relatively civil his tone was despite his seething anger. Maymi was his girlfriend. It didn't matter to him that she never accepted it. He did and that was the only thing that mattered.

She shot him a look of disdain. "I can't believe how protective you are being of the cupcake lady. You would have never done that for me, but that's okay. She's still worthless." Chloe snickered then turned away. Walking over to the door, she opened it and walked out slamming it closed behind her.

His mind refused to register Chloe's insults against Maymi because her words meant *nothing*.

A war of emotions raged within Jensen. The urge to rush over to Maymi's apartment and yank her into his arms had him rushing towards his office door, but he stopped himself before his hand touched the doorknob.

She wouldn't let him within touching distance of her. Not after hearing only part of his stupid comments weeks ago. Maymi had run out of the place so fast, and when he didn't go after her he knew it only fueled her wrong ideas about his true feelings.

Running Fitness 24 took up a huge part of his time, but it never filled up the emptiness that his heart until he found Maymi. Falling in love with her had come completely out of left field. He wasn't expecting to love her nearly as much as he did now. Yet, it was the best thing that had ever happened.

The first time he laid eyes on her, all he could think about was getting her away from his thriving business as fast as possible. However, the most important thing for him to do *now* was get Maymi back.

He knew he had hurt her because he still saw the pain on her face every time he closed his eyes at night. If he got...no, *when* he got Maymi back, he was going to work damn hard to make sure no one hurt her again including him.

❧❦

Standing out on the balcony of her apartment, Maymi held the drink in her hand staring blindly off into the distance. This part of the loft captivated her the moment she walked through the front door. She had been willing to pay extra for it but luckily she got this place at a steal from Tatum's parents.

It had taken her about two weeks to make Jazmaine and Tatum understand that she was strong enough to be by herself now. They had taken turns spending the nights with her and sometimes they were both here on the weekends. She still felt bad that Jazmaine cancelled her date with Akito to take care of her, but she was a mess the night of the break-in at Sinful.

Maymi didn't know what hurt worse, truly knowing that her business was a total loss, or hearing how happy Jensen was about it. She heard he had gotten the property at a steal because of the damage done to it. He had broken her heart.

She thought she wouldn't ever get over Hudson's death, but Jensen helped her see she could love again. However, he only did it to stab her in the back.

Bringing the glass to her mouth, she took a sip of the liquor swallowing it. She hoped it would numb some of the pain still in her heart, but nothing was helping her forget her time with Jensen. They had such a good chemistry that turned into more for her. She loved him... no, she had fallen in love with him.

How could he betray me so easily without even a second thought?

"Enough, you can't keep trying to figure him out," she whispered to herself. Jensen wasn't the man she believed and it was time for her to start letting go. Three weeks was long enough to be held up in this apartment drowning her sorrows in liquor and junk food. She had to find a way to shake it off and get back on track.

Turning around she went back into the apartment and was headed for the bedroom when her cell phone rang. Maymi slid her hand into the pocket of her robe and grabbed it.

"Hello," she answered.

"Please talk to me."

Maymi shivered at the sound of Jensen's deep voice on the other end. She hadn't heard his voice since that night because Jazmaine had been screening her phone calls.

"No, I don't think that would be a good idea. I can't deal with you right now...maybe never."

"Let me come and see you," he asked not giving up.

Walking over to the kitchen island, Maymi placed the glass down and took a seat. "No, I don't think that would be a good idea either. We have nothing to say to each other. By the way, congratulations on getting Sinful's old building. I heard the construction is about to start."

"Sweetheart, you don't know the entire story. There is so much I need to tell you. If I can't come to you, how about you come to me?" Jensen suggested. "I'm just at home working out. I really need to see you. We can't leave things like this between us."

"I hate you."

"I'll text you my address and I'll let the decision be yours," he said softly before hanging up.

Maymi pressed the end button on her phone. She tossed it down on the island then a few minutes later it beeped signaling she had gotten a text. Reaching for the phone, she picked it up and read Jensen's text. There was a message along with his address. A part of her wanted to ignore it and just pretend she hadn't heard his sexy voice on the phone. Yet, the other side of her wanted to go to his house and tell him to go to hell.

She only debated for a few minutes before she slid off the stool and made her way towards the front door. She wouldn't be able to move forward until she put Jensen in her past. He asked to see her and she was about to grant his wish.

Chapter Thirty-Nine

Hearing the doorbell, Jensen placed the weight down on the bench and left his personal gym next to his bedroom. Making his way down the long hallway, he went to the front door and answered it.

"Maymi," he said shocked.

He had given her his address, but he didn't think she would actually show up to his house. Seeing her after so many weeks was an instant turn-on for his body. She looked *so* gorgeous in her shirt and short denim skirt. All he could think about was stripping her and having his way with her.

"I hate the sight of you," Maymi screamed at him. "I never want to see you again. I just came over here to tell you to go to hell. Stay out of my life. I can do badly all by myself. I don't need you in the background shoving me in the wrong direction."

She reached out to slap him, but he grabbed her wrist jerking her hard against his chest. He had stood here for the last few minutes listening to her rant and he was done. He had something to say and she was going to listen to him. Jensen pulled her inside the house closing and locking the door behind her.

"Maymi, you need to calm down and listen to me. You don't even know what is going on."

"I understand perfectly. Now, let go of me," she yelled, pulling at her wrist.

"No."

Jensen picked Maymi up and carried her from the living room down the hallway toward his bedroom. He had tried to be nice and let her get her anger out of her system, but he was tired. This had been the longest three weeks he had ever lived through.

"I heard you telling Casper it might have been a good thing that

Sinful got destroyed. How could you say something so cruel? Put me down. God, I can't believe I actually thought I loved you."

Jensen stopped and stared down into Maymi's face. "Baby, I already love you and I think you love me too, but just are too blinded to admit it now. However, I plan to change all of that very soon." He kissed her on the lips before lifting his head and walking the remainder of the way to his bedroom.

Holding her against his chest, he opened the bedroom door and went through. Carrying her struggling body over to the bed, he laid her down on the bed and captured her mouth again with his cutting off anything else she wanted to tell him.

Grabbing her hot pink t-shirt, he ripped it down the middle and pulled it the rest of the way off Maymi's body. His fingers didn't waste any time unhooking the front of her white bra and taking it off her luscious body as well. He gave Maymi another long kiss before easing his lips away and raining kisses over her jaw and down her neck until he came to her full breasts.

He cupped one in his hand running his nail over the tip before blowing on it. Lowering his head, he slowly sucked the hard treat into his mouth.

"Jensen, I hate you," Maymi said then ruined it by moaning and running her fingers through his hair.

Smiling against the softness of her breasts, Jensen slid his down her body and with his left hand he unbuttoned Maymi's denim skirt. He pulled it down her thighs and rubbed his thumb over her pussy through her panties.

Lifting his head, he brought his mouth up to her ear. "Are you sure, sweetheart? Because, I think your body is telling me something different." He continued to brush his thumb over the damp spot already there making it wetter and wetter.

"Yes."

"Let me see if I can change that for you or more importantly me." He tugged her skirt and underwear the rest of the way off her sizzling body.

Jensen quickly stood up and untied his sweatpants slipping them off his body before rejoining Maymi back on the bed. Slipping a hand back between Maymi's thighs, he eased a finger into her tight pussy, loving how her body came alive for him.

"Tell me again how much you hate me. Tell me to stop and I'll do it, Maymi." He slid another finger inside of Maymi watching as she struggled to keep from moaning again, but he *knew* her body. He recognized she liked and she loved being touched.

"I would completely stop and let you get redressed. I wouldn't even try to stop you from leaving." Jensen increased the pace, shoving his finger even deeper inside of Maymi.

However, Maymi still didn't say a word to him. All she did was bite her bottom lip and grab the bedspread underneath them between her small hands. She wasn't going to win at this. He would get her to tell him that she wanted him.

"I can get you to answer me." Jensen withdrew his fingers and got off the bed.

Bending down, he slowly moved in and kissed Maymi's legs breathing in the scent that was only hers and no one else's. "Baby, you smell so fucking *good*."

He wanted to torture her, but being this close to her pussy was killing him. Without giving her any warning, he dived right into her sweet smelling, wet pussy. He licked and sucked at her clit until her body was about to come and then Jensen stopped.

"No!" Maymi whimpered, staring at him with lust-filled eyes.

"What are you saying to me, Maymi?" Jensen asked, looking up at Maymi from between her smooth, brown thighs. "Do you still hate me or do you want me? I'm confused. I need you to clear it up for me."

"I—"

"Say it. Tell me what you need from me and baby, I'll give it to you."

"I want you to fuck me. I need to you do it," she said, staring him directly in the eyes.

Those weren't exactly the words Jensen wanted to hear from his woman's lips, but his cock ached too much to argue with her. Sliding his way back up her body, he rubbed his cock over her pussy and pushed inside until he was fully inside of her tight, welcoming heat.

Jensen planted kisses along Maymi's neck as he began thrusting in and out of her. "Maymi, I love you," he whispered against her skin. "You are everything to me and I'm going to prove it to you."

"Yes," she cried. Her fingers slid up and down his damp back as he buried himself further into her. Seconds later, Maymi's orgasms ripped through her body as her pussy stroked his hard cock.

His own release coming, Jensen covered Maymi's mouth with his as he started fucking her with hard, quick thrusts until he tore his mouth away and hollered as his seed shot deep inside of her tight pussy.

Chapter Forty

Something cool landing on Maymi's chest woke her up from her light sleep; she opened her eyes and glanced down noticing a set of keys on her breasts. Picking them up, she looked over at Jensen and found him watching her.

"What is this?" she asked, holding them up.

"They are for you," he answered, kissing her on the mouth.

Maymi leaned away from him. They might have just had sex but it didn't mean they were back together. She shouldn't have fallen asleep in the first place. She had come over here for an entirely different reason, but as soon as Jensen touched her mind had gotten scrambled and she couldn't think of anything else but being with him one more time.

"I don't understand," she said, sitting up in the bed. "I don't need a set of keys. Look, I really should go. This was a bad idea." Maymi tried to move away from Jensen, but he pulled her back against his chest.

"No, I let you walk away from me once but I'll be damned if I'll be dumb enough to let it happen again."

Sighing, Maymi pulled the covers around her body and looked at him. "We can't go back to the way things were. Too much has happened between us. I know we just had sex, but this doesn't change anything.

"First, we didn't just have sex and I don't want you to ever say that again to me," he corrected. "Another thing is you misheard what I was telling Casper and before I could tell you, Jazmaine and Tatum were into our business."

She wasn't going to let him lie his way out of this. "Jensen, you said it was a good thing Sinful got destroyed. It was the best thing for the both of us."

"Yes, I did but there was more to it."

"What more could they have been?" Maymi demanded.

"Do you want to know what those keys are for?" Jensen asked, glancing down at them and then back up at her.

"No, of course not."

"They are to Health Pro. I bought it weeks ago for Casper to have his own personal gym, but as usual he decided he wasn't interested in that much responsibility. So, I was left with this huge piece of prime real estate without any real use for it until Sinful got destroyed."

Slowly, she began to realize what Jensen was telling her. "Are you telling me that you are giving me Health Pro to start a new bakery?" she whispered.

"What you overheard me telling Casper my thoughts about it," Jensen answered. "I think it's the perfect spot for you. I will even help you interview people to help you out. Maymi, I love you so damn much. I wouldn't ever get any enjoyment out of your pain.

"I wanted to tell you about this way before now, but your friends had you locked away like gold in Fort Knox and I couldn't get to you." Cupping her face in his hands, Jensen stared into her eyes. "I know you screamed you hated me earlier. Is that really true?"

Tears fell down her cheeks hitting the back of Jensen's hands as she shook her head. "No, I love you. I hated that I did especially when I thought you loved that my bakery got destroyed, but I did. I still can't believe you're handing the keys of an entire building over to me. I can put a picture of my grandmother on the wall now."

"Baby, you can do anything you like. It's all yours. I'm just so thrilled I didn't lose you," Jensen whispered and lowered his head to kiss her but she moved back. "What's wrong?"

"I just have one question before I let you kiss me," Maymi said.

"Alright, what is it?" He took the keys from her hand and tossed them on the stand next to the bed. He slowly lowered her back down to the bed and covered her body with his.

"Will you be my assistant at least two times a week? I mean if you going to be with me you'll at least need to know how to make two different desserts."

"Maymi, if they are sinful as you are than I will make it there three days a week," Jensen agreed right before he kissed her.

The End

About the Author

The Queen of Tease: If you want to read interracial romance stories that leaves you panting for more and turning the pages faster than you can read them. Marie is for you.

After reading her first "dirty" book as a teenager, Marie knew she had to become a writer. She started writing a few years ago because she wanted to reach for her dream. She writes her characters so her fans will believe in the Happily Ever After. She loves collecting bear figurines and reading a HOT book when she gets the chance.

Find out more about Marie here:
Official Site: http://marierochelle.weebly.com/
Official Blog: http://shopdiva28.blogspot.com/
Yahoo group: http://groups.yahoo.com/group/marie_rochelle/
Yahoo discussion group: http://groups.yahoo.com/group/MarieRochelle2/?yguid=289462859

CPSIA information can be obtained at www.ICGtesting.com
Printed in the USA
BVOW03s1316140414

350483BV00001B/25/P